RED DIANA

Susan Alexander

"Children are the anchors that hold a mother to life."

Sophocles, *Phaedra*

"Romance fails us and so do friendships, but the relationship of parent and child...remains indelible and indestructible, the strongest relationship on earth."

Theodor Reik, *Of Love and Lust* (1957)

"A man that studieth revenge keeps his own wounds green, which otherwise would heal and do well."

Francis Bacon, "On Revenge," *Essays* (1625)

Chapter 1

They found her, trembling and icy cold, leaning against a dirty brick wall in a corner of the parking lot behind a rusty Ford minivan. Her matchstick legs tucked beneath her, she looked like a small frightened animal, quivering on the filthy asphalt pavement.

"Here! She's over here!" Abby shouted.

Karen raced over to her shivering daughter. Abby was hovering over her, clutching Davi's hands. "Get the blanket, she's freezing!" Abby said. Karen ran back to the Camry for Abby's blanket.

Abby was helping Davi to her feet when Karen approached with the blanket, thrusting it at Abby, who quickly threw it over the eight-year-old's slight body. Karen felt paralyzed, unable to help.

"Okay, Davi, everything's okay," Abby said, clutching the tiny blanketed figure. "Come with us now. We're taking you home."

Davi allowed Abby to shepherd her through the parking lot, past the rusty minivan, to Abby's late-model Camry. Abby gently guided Davi into the back seat, then nudged her inside still farther. Karen slid into the seat beside her small daughter and put her arm around Davi, hugging her tightly while Abby climbed into the driver's seat and steered the car out of the parking lot.

Davi's eyes opened wide, staring glassily through the car's dirty windows at the city, sodden and gray in the early-morning chill. Karen forced herself to say something. "You're okay now, Davi," she said, her voice trembling. "You're okay. You'll be home very soon."

Chapter 2

Karen Clark stared out the window of her 14th-floor office. The gray building facing her was barely distinct from the gray sky surrounding it. *San Francisco on an August morning: gray on gray.*

The grayness enveloping her matched her somber mood. *Davi is home again, yes, but she's practically catatonic.*

Two weeks after her abduction, Davi was still badly shaken. Not surprising, Karen thought. Being grabbed outside of the 7-Eleven like that, pushed into a nondescript car, taken somewhere…somewhere she couldn't even talk about. Not yet, anyway.

What had Vera Haglund said? It might be months before Davi could tell anyone all the details of her abduction.

Davi was with Vera now, while Karen spent a few minutes in her office checking her stack of files. She'd return home soon, in time to spend the rest of the day with Davi.

Karen's focus right now was helping Davi get over her trauma, helping her to sleep and eat. Taking her to see Vera, her therapist, three times a week.

Abby and the other partners were giving Karen space, allowing her to spend all the time she needed to help Davi get back to some semblance of normal. Karen needed that time, too.

"If he did anything to harm her, I'll kill him," Karen had told Greg Chan when he showed up at her apartment the day after Davi was abducted. Her usually smooth forehead was furrowed, her usually full mouth set in a grim line.

Davi was still asleep. "I'm serious," Karen added. "I'll track him down and kill him...."

"But you know there was no demand for ransom. And the doctors said she wasn't harmed physically," Chan said. The San Francisco detective was impassive. His handsome Asian features, topped by a thatch of jet black hair, showed no emotion whatsoever.

Why doesn't he seem to care about this case?

"Not a bruise, nothing," he added.

"But the trauma, Greg. What she's gone through mentally, emotionally...." Karen's voice quavered. She couldn't bear to think about it. The terror Davi must have felt....

And what did that goddamned note mean? That note, pinned to her t-shirt. "You're next, Karen." What the hell did that mean?

Karen sighed.

What did this pervert want? To terrify a little girl? To abduct me next? Why?

And if he wanted to abduct me, why did he grab Davi first, then release her with that note pinned to her shirt? Why not grab me in the first place?

"You're next, Karen." The words on the note, written in a nearly indecipherable scrawl on a torn-off scrap of generic white paper, haunted Karen.

What exactly have I done? What did I do in my lousy 40 years on this planet to inspire some nut to do this? Damn it, I'm a lawyer, and I can't even protect my own kid, my own helpless little kid, from all the crazies who walk the streets of San Francisco.

Filled with anger, Karen turned away from Greg Chan. His failure to offer any concrete help left her feeling despondent. Sensing Karen's unhappiness with him, Greg quietly left her apartment, muttering softly "I'll get back to you."

Karen pushed her reddish-brown hair away from her face, her gray-green eyes reflecting the guilt she felt.

I never should have let Davi come downtown. I should have known better.

Sure, she begged and pleaded to come downtown with me. And what else was she going to do on a weekday in mid-August, with day camp over and nothing else in the offing that day?

But I should have said no. I should have found some other place for her. Some place other than my office. I should have kept calling, calling to arrange a play date at the home of a friend from school. A friend with a stay-at-home mom. A mom who'd have taken better care of her than I did.

Back in her apartment, Karen paced back and forth in her living room, waiting for Vera's call.

If I just hadn't let her go downstairs to the 7-Eleven for M&M's. She'd insisted on taking the elevator by herself—"C'mon, Mom, I can do it, please, Mom, please" she pleaded—and she never came back.

Fifteen minutes went by, then twenty, before Karen finally glanced at her watch and frantically rushed out to look for her daughter.

No Davi.

Karen ran into the 7-Eleven where she suspected Davi had gone. No one remembered seeing her, a diminutive eight-year-old with curly blond hair, wearing a pair of washed-out jeans and a bright green hoodie.

Karen had rushed back to her office and called the police. When they arrived fifteen minutes later, they couldn't offer much help. Just stay by the phone, they told Karen. Just wait for a call. If the caller stays on the line long enough, we'll try to trace it.

Karen slept in her office that night, sitting upright in her black leather chair. Tried to sleep, anyway. With Abby Plummer staying just down the hall, Karen sat in her chair all night, frantic, waiting for a call, unsure whether the abductor would call at her office or her apartment. She rarely used her cell phone and doubted that anyone even knew the number.

Every ten minutes, she checked her home answering machine, just to make sure.

The call finally came on her office phone at 7:47 a.m. A distorted voice, muttering into a phone somewhere: "Your daughter's in the parking lot at Broadway and Front Street. Two blocks from the Embarcadero."

"Who are you? Why are you doing this?" Karen screamed into the phone. "Why...?"

The caller hung up before she could finish her question. Karen slammed the phone down and raced down the hall. "Abby, he just called!"

Abby looked up from her computer, her blue eyes widening under her dark brown bangs. "Thank God! Where is she?"

"A parking lot. A parking lot on Broadway, near the Embarcadero. Do you know where that is?"

"Sure, I used to work around there." Abby jumped up and put her arms around Karen. "Don't worry now, Karen. She must be okay, or he wouldn't have left her there."

"I don't know…I don't know. She could be hurt…she could…she could…."

"Don't worry! I'm sure she's all right," Abby said. "Let's get my car and get over there right away."

Chapter 3

The apartment phone rang, startling Karen. She'd returned to her apartment and was trying to make sense of a legal document while Davi was with Vera Haglund. But Karen was just reading the same words over and over, unable to concentrate.

"It's Vera, Karen."

Karen froze. "How's she doing?"

"Better. Much better."

Karen's heart skipped a beat. Davi was doing better.

"Can we meet somewhere? Just for a few minutes?" Vera asked.

"Sure," Karen said. "I can meet you near your office. But what about Davi?"

"She can stay here for a while. My partner's in the office. Davi can look at some of the kids' books in our waiting room."

"Good," Karen said. "How's Caffé Union?"

"Perfect. I'll be there in ten minutes."

Karen rushed out of her apartment, heading on foot to Union Street and the coffee shop close to both her apartment and Vera's office. Vera was waiting, a mug of coffee on the table in front of her, when Karen arrived.

She ordered coffee and focused on Vera, waiting for her to speak.

"Good news, Karen," Vera said. "She's starting to respond. I think we've made a bit of a breakthrough." The therapist, recommended by the SFPD, was about 60, with a trim figure, a short blonde haircut, and a pleasant oval face. A face that now looked happier than it had the last time Karen saw her.

"A breakthrough?" Karen's heart started beating faster when she heard that word. *Could there really be a breakthrough?*

"She's starting to remember things. She remembers a couple of things in the room where she slept that night...."

"Oh my God! What? What did she say?"

"Well, it's not much to go on, but it's a start."

"Yes?"

"She remembers sleeping on a brown sofa."

A brown sofa? There had to be thousands of brown sofas in San Francisco. A clue like that was probably useless.

"Anything else?"

"Well, yes," Vera said. Her voice sounded uncertain. "It doesn't make much sense. At least not yet. Not till she can remember even more."

Vera paused. Karen's patience was beginning to wear thin. *What is it? Just tell me!*

"Yes, Vera," she said, trying to keep her voice under control. "What did she say?"

"Red Diana."

"What?"

"Red Diana."

"You mean red, the color red?"

"Apparently."

"And Diana, the name Diana?"

"That's what she said, Karen. She even spelled it for me: D-I-A-N-A."

Karen was dumbstruck. "Red Diana." *What did it mean?*

Was the abductor a woman? A woman with red hair? Or one who wore a red sweater? Maybe she had a florid face—a face Davi might describe as "red"?

Or was this woman just one in a gang of abductors? The one the gang assigned to watch little girls?

Karen tried to think. *Did the words mean something else entirely? Was it the name of a place, maybe a street? Was there a street in San Francisco named "Diana"?*

Karen knew some streets in the city had women's names. Octavia Street in Karen's neighborhood. And one in the Mission. Dolores. Was there a Diana Street somewhere in the city?

"Karen?" Vera was saying. "Are you still with me?"

"Yes, yes, of course. I just…I just don't know what it could mean."

"Neither do I. But I'll tell the police what she said. Maybe they can come up with some leads based on it."

"Yes, tell the police, by all means," Karen said quickly. "Tell Greg Chan right away."

Maybe the police would know what it meant. Maybe they already had a file on this person, this Red Diana.

It was something, at least. After two full weeks, it was something.

11

Chapter 4

Karen's second meeting with Greg Chan went better than the first. She'd asked him to meet her at her law firm's office on Market Street. The sun was shining that morning through the large window facing the busy street.

A good omen? Karen hoped it was.

She was still extremely nervous--worried about Davi, and worried about herself as well. She tried to eat a healthy diet, especially in front of Davi, but she had very little appetite for food, and her slim figure had grown even slimmer. She kept her masses of reddish-brown hair under minimal control with a barrette she sometimes stashed in her desk drawer. But she had no desire to comb her hair, to check her overall appearance in the mirror. Too much else to worry about.

She'd returned to work part-time. The law firm's partners heard the whole story from Abby and understood Karen's need to resume some sort of normal existence.

Davi was back at Sheraton School, beginning the new school year at the elementary school near Karen's apartment where Davi had been happy the previous year. She seemed comfortable back in the familiar pattern of school and home.

"I like third grade," Davi announced after her first day. "Ms. Hamilton is really nice. She reminds me of Rosemary."

Karen was relieved to hear these reassuring words. Rosemary Carter had been their kind next-door neighbor when they lived in Evanston.

Juanita Perez, Davi's trusted sitter, picked her up after school on the days Karen worked, and stayed with her until Karen returned home. Juanita was a savvy USF student taking a semester break from her studies, and Karen had been delighted to find her. Things were possibly returning to some semblance of normal.

When Greg arrived at Karen's office, his initial brusqueness appeared to have worn off. He seemed more sympathetic, more connected to Davi's case.

But he wasn't particularly encouraging. "We've tried to track down some witnesses, Karen. Talked to as many people who were in the area as we could find. But no one recalls seeing this guy anywhere near the 7-Eleven. None of the employees could identify anyone in the store who was especially sketchy. A couple of homeless types, but they're generally harmless."

"What about outside the store? On Market Street? Lots of people must have been passing by...."

"Right. The problem is that everyone on that street is rushing, heading for some destination or other. Very few people pay attention to what's happening around them. We haven't found anyone who noticed anything unusual."

"No one saw this monster grab a little girl?"

"No one has come forward to report anything like an abduction, Karen. I know it's hard to believe, but people on a busy street like that are focused on themselves. Not really looking around at anything else."

Karen sighed. "What else are you doing?"

"There's not much we can do, Karen. Remember, he returned her unharmed. If we find him, we can charge him with kidnapping, and of course that's a serious charge. But we have homicides we're dealing with," Greg said, his dark eyes looking deeply into Karen's. "Kids who've been shot. Or raped. This can't take priority over cases like that."

"I know that, Greg," Karen said. Her heart speeded up as she thought about what had happened to her daughter. No, it wasn't rape or murder. But what happened had traumatized her. "I know that," she repeated. "But...but we can't let this madman get away with it.... What if he tries to grab her again? What if he comes after me next?" Karen had to confront Greg with the terrible worry she faced every day. "He knows my name. Davi wasn't just a random target. Can we bring in the FBI? We have to find this man."

"When your call first came in, we thought about contacting the FBI," Greg said, his face reflecting what he remembered about that call. "We were about to call them, maybe get their CARD Team involved, when you called to tell us your daughter had been returned to you unharmed. At that point, we dropped the idea of bringing in the FBI. But...," he paused. "It's somewhat late in the game, but I can ask my supervisor if we should look into that now."

"Yes, yes, do that," Karen said. *The FBI's CARD Team? Is that something I should know about?*

"In the meantime, Karen, let's review what we know." Greg pulled out his worn spiral notebook, filled with handwritten notes. "Your daughter...Davi...she remembers what? Being grabbed from behind as she left the 7-Eleven. She thinks it was a man, but she couldn't see his face. He covered her eyes with a piece of cloth and pushed her into the back seat of a car. She was scared, but he told her you wanted him to take her somewhere. That you'd be angry if she gave him any trouble. So she tried to lie there quietly. He drove her someplace, pushed her up some stairs, then put her in a room she can't describe very well and left her there alone overnight. Right?"

"Right," Karen nodded, her heart pounding as Greg continued to go through his notes.

"She can't remember much more than that till the next morning, when he pushed her back down the stairs and into the car, then dropped her off where you found her. She says he wore some sort of large mask covering his face, so she can't describe what he looks like. Right?'

"Yes."

"Also...she slept on a brown sofa. Right?

"Right."

"What else? Oh yeah," Greg said, reviewing his notes. "She remembers the words 'Red Diana.' Right?"

"That's right." Karen paused before going on. "Greg, I've been thinking about those two words. Are there any streets called 'Diana' in San Francisco? Could that be a possible clue?"

"Streets named Diana?"

"Lots of streets have women's names. Dolores...."

"I'll look into it," Greg said.

Karen wondered how much time he'd actually devote to it. But one day later, Greg got back to Karen. "Nothing new on your case, Karen. But there *is* a street called Diana."

"There is?" Karen's heart jumped. Maybe that would lead somewhere.

"I checked all the streets in San Francisco. Diana...it's a very short street in the Bayview. Right near our Bayview station, actually. It's only one long block, with about 15 houses. We have a couple of guys going door-to-door, making inquiries at every house. I'll let you know if I hear anything."

Karen felt hopeful for the first time in weeks. Maybe the abductor lived right there on Diana Street. Maybe the police could track him down, tie him somehow to the color red, get him to admit his culpability.

It would be hard to wait. Very hard.

Chapter 5

Imelda Bennett looked sad. *As sad as I must have looked four years ago*, Karen thought, looking across the conference table at the firm's new client, the plump white-haired Mrs. Bennett. A widow who really loved her husband. A widow who wasn't just going through the motions, pretending to be sad, when all she cared about was the size of her dead husband's estate.

Karen was grateful for the distraction. Nearly a month after Davi's abduction, with the police investigation not making much headway, Karen welcomed the need to focus on something besides Davi. Thankfully, Davi was doing well back at school, and life was returning to quasi-normal for both of them, Karen trying desperately to push her fears out of her mind as much as she could.

And now I have to help Abby get the Bennett estate in shape, whether Mrs. Bennett loved her husband or not. That's my job.

Still, she reminds me of somebody.

Karen spent the next half-hour with Abby and Mrs. Bennett, going through the particulars of the Bennett estate. Finally the three women rose and headed out of the conference room. As Karen said goodbye at the elevator, shaking the older woman's hand, she suddenly remembered the woman who resembled Mrs. Bennett.

Of course! Vivienne Schreiber! How could I forget? My first client at my first job after law school. First-year associate at Garrity & Costello in New York.

Karen could barely recall the work she'd had to do for Vivienne Schreiber. Something about setting up a trust, wasn't it? The white-haired Mrs. Schreiber had been enormously wealthy, the widow of one of the firm's big-bucks clients, but she'd been a placid and easy-to-please client. No trouble at all. Just like Mrs. Bennett.

Karen grabbed a Diet Coke in the kitchen and returned to her office. *God, I haven't thought about Garrity & Costello in years! Almost forgot how much I hated it there.*

Working with Mrs. Schreiber wasn't typical. *An aberration from the routine I fell into a few months later. The corporate practice I grew to hate, with its overwhelming burden of billable hours, its inhospitable partners who never smiled at me, its legions of mean-spirited clients who were always ready to screw the little guy.*

I learned a lot there, I'll say that for it. But I wouldn't go back to that kind of firm for any amount of money. Never.

*   *   *

Karen had set her sights on becoming a lawyer at an early age. It had been lonely as an only child growing up in a two-story colonial in Summit, New Jersey. Neighborhood kids weren't much company for a brainy kid like Karen. She preferred to be alone, reading or copying pictures of horses from her favorite books.

Summers and school holidays, her mother would drive the Olds into downtown Newark, where the trip always ended with a hotly anticipated elevator ride to her father's law office. Karen remembered her father looking oh-so-important, sitting behind a massive oak desk, either too busy to talk to her, or else making a huge fuss over her, telling his overworked secretary that his 'little princess" had arrived.

Karen decided at age twelve to pattern herself after her father. To become a lawyer and have her own paper-strewn office where *she* would sit behind a massive desk, looking oh-so-important. She soon discovered that being brainy would help her get there. After graduating at the top of her high school class, Karen went on to Princeton, then Harvard Law. And Harvard had led to Garrity & Costello, where her grandiose illusions about the glamorous practice of law sadly and dishearteningly faded.

* * *

Two hours later, Karen packed up her things and headed for home. On her way out, she ran into Ramsey Boyd, a new associate at the firm. She'd met him only briefly at a lunch meeting in the firm's conference room. Smiling, she tried skirting him en route to the elevator.

"Hey, Karen," he said, blocking her. "Great to see you. How're you doin'?" he grinned.

Ram was tall, good-looking, with a shock of light brown hair. He might have appealed to her under other circumstances, but his silly grin struck Karen as somewhat creepy. Why was he blocking her this way? And why the uber-casual tone? Didn't he know the trauma she'd been dealing with? Was he trying to make light of it? Or was he simply so socially inept that he didn't know how to approach her?

"I'm okay, Ram. How're you?"

"I'm great, Karen," he said, his eyes narrowing to scrutinize her better. "Want to get a drink?"

"Sorry, Ram," Karen said quickly. "Gotta run or I'll miss my bus."

He paused, trying to decide whether she was being honest or simply chose to reject him outright. "Another time?"

Karen hesitated. It wouldn't hurt to meet him for coffee. Better than having a drink with him after work. "Sure. Let's have coffee sometime," she said.

Ram's face brightened at her suggestion. "Great. I'll drop by your office, okay?"

Karen nodded. She pushed past him and hastily made her way to the elevator. Her abrupt encounter with Ramsey Boyd left her feeling uncomfortable. She wanted to learn more about him before things went any further.

A few minutes later, Karen was crammed into the crowded 45 bus heading towards her apartment on the border of Pacific Heights. Her thoughts drifted back to the three years she'd spent at Garrity & Costello. She'd suppressed most of the unpleasantness she experienced there, but what if she could resurrect some of it? Could that possibly help?

Help her figure out what had led to Davi's abduction? And the note pinned to Davi's shirt?

Chapter 6

Karen slowly stirred her decaf skim latte. *Why would anyone do this to Davi? He had to be a madman....*

"What are you thinking, Karen?"

Karen looked up at Abby, sitting across from her in the crowded Starbucks just down Market Street from their office. Abby's blue eyes were filled with concern for Karen.

"This person, this person who took Davi. He—or she—had to be insane, don't you think?" Karen said. "To terrify a small child that way, to…"

"Absolutely. Only a truly disturbed person could do it. But you just said 'he or she.' Do you think it might be a woman?" Abby slowly took a sip of her chai latte.

"I suppose it could be a woman," Karen said. "But the voice on the phone, it sounded like a man's voice. And Davi's pretty sure a man grabbed her."

"Must have been a man," Abby nodded. "I can't see a woman doing that to a child."

"He must have wanted to hurt *me* somehow," Karen said. "He put that note on her shirt—'You're next, Karen.'" Karen felt a chill, just saying those three words.

Abby nodded. They hadn't noticed the note, hidden by Davi's green hoodie, when they found her in the parking lot. Their first priority was getting her home as fast as possible.

But once they were home and pulled off her hoodie, they saw the note pinned to her shirt. "Why would this guy want to hurt you, Karen?" Abby said, looking puzzled.

"Why would he put that note on Davi's shirt? Do you think his real target was you?"

"I don't know." Karen had asked herself that question a thousand times. *What enemies have I made--enemies who'd hate me enough to do this?*

"Everyone at the firm is crazy about you," Abby assured her. "We're all horrified by what happened. You need to tell us how we can help...."

Karen's thoughts drifted to Jon. He would have been appalled. *I've failed our darling Davi.*

In her mind's eye, Karen could see Jon's face. The hazel eyes, the shiny brown hair, the smile that lit up every room he entered. *Jon...Jon, if only you were here with me now....*

Karen suddenly sat upright. If Jon *were* here.... *He was so smart, so intuitive, he'd think of something. He'd know exactly what to do.*

"Karen?" Abby was staring at her, a puzzled look on her face. "Are you okay?"

"Yes, I'm fine. I was just wondering. How would Jon deal with this?"

"Jon?"

"Jon. Jon Smith, my husband."

"Oh." Abby nodded, trying to recall what Karen had told her about Jon.

Karen knew she had to focus, really focus. *What <u>would</u> Jon do right now? He'd know what to do.*

"So you're trying to think what Jon would do now?" Abby asked tentatively.

"Right…." Karen's voice drifted off, her eyes glazing over as she concentrated. She couldn't help thinking of the acronym "WWJD," and she nearly smiled. But the situation was too awful to smile.

Jon…Jon would have kept his head. He would have used his analytic mind to figure things out.

Oh, how I miss Jon right now.

Abby slowly rose from the table. "I'm so sorry, Karen. I wish I could do something to help," she said quietly as she exited Starbucks, leaving Karen alone with her melancholy thoughts.

Chapter 7

Karen was sifting through a pile of dusty file folders when Abby entered her office the next morning.

"Can I help?" Abby asked.

"I don't think so," Karen said.

"What are you looking for? Are those our files?"

The legal-sized folders looked ancient to Abby. No one at Franklin & Cooper had used those in years.

"They're from Garrity & Costello. The New York firm where I worked right after law school. Remember?"

Abby looked uncertain. "No, not really."

"Sorry. I thought I told you about Melissa Cohen. My secretary in New York. She probably wasn't supposed to, but she made copies of my case files for the three years I worked there. After I left the firm and moved to Chicago, she sent them to me, and I threw them into a file cabinet. One of the file cabinets I moved here from Chicago last year.

"I haven't looked at them since Melissa sent them years ago."

"And now you have a case that's related to one of them?" Abby asked.

"Not exactly," Karen said, flipping through the yellowing folders.

"Then what?"

Karen looked up, a weary look on her face. "I couldn't sleep last night. I kept thinking there had to be a reason why someone grabbed Davi...."

Abby waited.

"I started thinking about my old cases, the ones I worked on at Garrity. Maybe I angered somebody there...."

"Why there? Why not here?"

"Oh, Abby, there's a world of difference between Garrity and this place. At Garrity, we trampled on people all the time. We were totally focused on preserving the wealth of our own clients. We didn't care what happened to the people on the other side. Our practice here is a lot different. A lot more humane. Even more than the work I did at Stein & Walter in Chicago. Here we handle estates and trusts, real estate deals. We look out for our clients, sure, but we usually wind up negotiating with the other side. We don't decimate our opponents the way we did at Garrity."

"So now you're thinking you made some enemies at Garrity?"

"Maybe. I don't know."

"How many years since you left?" Abby seated herself in one of the chairs that faced Karen's desk.

"About twelve...." Twelve years away from that sweatshop, Karen thought. *Thank God I had the guts to leave when I did.*

"Well," Abby said, her blue eyes focused on Karen, "twelve years is a long time. If you really got on someone's shit list while you were there, why would he wait till now to go after you?"

Karen hesitated. She'd considered that already. The twelve-year gap did cast doubt on her newborn theory. "I don't know," she said. "I...I'm trying to figure that one out."

Abby stood up to leave. "Have to get back to my desk now. Derek may be looking for me." Abby worked closely with Derek Cooper, another one of the partners. Like Abby and Karen, he was about 40, but unlike Karen, he focused on the firm's high-stakes real-estate deals, sometimes with Abby's assistance.

"Right. Go ahead," Karen said, turning back to the file folders. "I just want to look through these files another minute or two."

Before Abby could leave Karen's office, Ramsey Boyd stuck his head in the doorway. "Can we have coffee later today?" he asked hopefully, a broad smile covering his face.

"Oh, Ram, I'm swamped right now," Karen said, gesturing at the pile of folders in front of her. "Maybe tomorrow."

Ram's face changed fast. A dejected look replaced the smile he'd had a moment earlier. He turned and quickly walked away.

"What's up with Ram?" Abby asked. "Are you seeing him?"

"No, I'm not. He just seems interested...."

Abby paused. "Watch your step with him, Karen," she said. "Someone told me he has a sketchy history with women. You're probably better off not getting started with him."

Karen couldn't help wondering what Abby meant, but Abby scooted out the door before she could ask. Questions about Ram would have to wait.

Immersing herself in the old files again, Karen went backward in time, beginning with the cases she'd worked on last, just before leaving Garrity. It seemed hopeless, searching for something that might somehow be connected to Davi's abduction.

Whose life did I ruin, who hates me enough to do this?

So many cases, so many damaged plaintiffs. Garrity & Costello had made its reputation by aggressively defending high-net-worth, high-profile clients. Mostly corporate work. Karen had been forced to focus on the mind-numbing corporate matters the partners wanted her to handle. Hardly any work fell outside that category.

As she sorted through the dusty files, Karen cringed, recalling the unpleasantness of her role at Garrity & Costello. Of using the tremendous resources of the big firm to defeat the claims of the little guys represented by marginal sole practitioners with limited resources. Little guys who never had a chance. *Luckily, I was able to avoid handling many cases like those.*

Still, how could I work at a place like that? Sure, everybody told me to put in a few years at one of the big firms, to get that kind of experience. But how did I spend three years working there and still sleep at night? I remember thinking that I couldn't breathe, that my soul was shrinking.

No wonder I took off for Walden...and the new life I hoped to begin there.

Chapter 8

Day after tedious day, Karen took a few minutes away from her work and painstakingly went through the pile of dusty files from Garrity & Costello. But nothing in those files led anywhere. She couldn't find a single thing that pointed in the direction of a disgruntled client. Nearly all of it had all been corporate work, one massive corporation up against another one, and no one individual seemed to be the unhappy victim of anything Karen had done.

"Have you found something?" Abby asked one morning, peering into Karen's office on her way down the hall to her own.

"Nothing," Karen said. "It's been a huge waste of time." Karen's face reflected how discouraged she felt, learning nothing that could help track down Davi's abductor.

Abby shook her head in sympathy. "Hmm.... What about your work at that Chicago firm?" she asked. "Stein and...what was it?"

"Stein & Walter," Karen said, pausing to think about Abby's suggestion. "You're right, Abby. I should look into my cases there. Even though most of them involved estate-planning, maybe there were some others, especially when I first started there." Karen dimly recalled being asked to do some extremely boring research, writing memos for the partners on a host of random subjects until she proved herself and could move into estate-planning, the field she preferred. "Maybe, if I could get my hands on those files, they would lead somewhere...."

"Let me know if I can do anything to help," Abby offered, going down the hall to her office.

Karen sat back in her chair and tried to focus on her tenure at Stein & Walter. She'd begun there in 1994, after she and Jon left Walden, Wisconsin, and moved together to Chicago.

Karen and Jon had met in the small town of Walden a few months earlier. For Karen, life there came to mean two things: the joy of meeting Jon and the near-death horror she endured thanks to someone she'd never suspected of harming her.

Karen had impulsively left her life in New York in the summer of 1993 and was working as a lawyer at a small firm in Walden when she met Jon, a bright young physician. They soon discovered they had Harvard in common. Jon had attended the college a few years before Karen turned up at the law school.

They compared notes, discovering that they'd both loved being students in Cambridge. They laughed about movies they'd both seen in Harvard Square and commiserated over their years-apart attempts to master ice skating at the hockey rink made famous in "Love Story."

Karen finished at the law school in 1990 and began working at Garrity & Costello while Jon had left Cambridge a few years earlier to get his M.D. in Wisconsin and complete a residency in pediatrics at Wash U in St. Louis.

When they met, Jon was working solo in the general practice started by his father, who'd retired and moved to Sarasota. But Jon had always hoped to specialize in pediatrics, so when he was recruited to join a busy pediatrics practice in Chicago, he was tempted to leave Walden and finally achieve his goal of becoming a pediatrician.

Meanwhile, Karen was traumatized by her near-fatal confrontation in a town where she'd hoped to pursue an idyllic life. She planned to leave Walden and return to her unfulfilling existence in New York. She didn't think she had a realistic option to do anything else.

But everything changed when Jon asked her to come with him to Chicago. She called Melissa, her secretary in New York, and told her she couldn't return to New York just then. "Not for a couple of weeks," Karen said, planning to spend that time with Jon, getting to know him better.

At the end of those two weeks, Karen knew she wanted to spend the rest of her life with Jon.

It turned out to be an easy choice. She'd been increasingly weary with her life in New York. Aside from her work at Garrity & Costello--work she hated--she disliked so many other things about life in the city. The crowds, the dirt, the noise. The rudeness she encountered almost everywhere. Not to mention a boyfriend who'd been cheating on her. Walden had been a pleasant respite from all that.

And now Jon had serendipitously appeared in her life. He was kind, caring, and totally devoted to Karen. She happily discovered that his enthusiasm, his excitement about treating the small patients he'd be seeing at his new practice, was infectious. It made Karen want to change her own life, to look ahead to a different career-path, one she would genuinely enjoy.

Deciding to make a fresh start in Chicago with Jon, Karen called Melissa to tell her she wouldn't be returning to Garrity & Costello after all. She asked her to collect whatever Karen had left behind in New York and send it to her. She'd let Melissa know her new address as soon as she could.

*   *   *

A few weeks later, Karen and Jon left Walden together and headed for Chicago. They found a tiny but surprisingly charming apartment on a quiet street near Lincoln Park. After one short month living together, Jon asked Karen to marry him. She said "yes" on the spot.

Karen's mother had died of breast cancer while Karen was still in college. So her father, David, now remarried in Tucson, came alone to witness Karen's wedding to Jon at Chicago's City Hall. After the wedding, Karen plunged into studying for the Illinois bar exam while Jon put in long hours seeing his young patients.

Once she passed the bar exam and was admitted to practice, she secured a job at Stein & Walter, a medium-sized firm on LaSalle Street in downtown Chicago, working there full-time until she gave birth to their daughter in 1997.

Karen and Jon named their small daughter Davida in memory of Karen's father, who'd died a year earlier. She soon became Davi (pronounced like Davey), a tiny and beloved addition to their family.

Searching for a home for their growing family, Karen and Jon found a close-to-perfect house near Central Street in Evanston. It was conveniently located near Jon's practice, which had moved to Evanston, and the nearby train station enabled Karen to get downtown in minutes.

Both of them relished the diversity they encountered in Evanston and the cultural offerings at nearby Northwestern University, where they found themselves attending theatrical and musical performances by the immensely talented students and the occasional celebrity performers. Often, they traveled a short distance to the neighboring suburb of Wilmette, where they feasted on mouth-watering omelets and apple pancakes at Walker Brothers Pancake House and viewed a wide range of movies at the downtown Wilmette movie theater.

After all of the angst Karen had experienced as a lawyer in New York, as well as her traumatic experience in Walden, she found her new home and the neighborhood surrounding it remarkably pleasant. She was especially delighted to encounter Rosemary and Sid Carter, friendly neighbors who lived next door on one side of the house. The neighbors on the other side were longtime residents who viewed Karen and Jon as nouveau-riche upstarts and chose largely to ignore them.

After Davi arrived, the management at Stein & Walter allowed Karen to work part-time, specializing in her preferred field, estate-planning. Following her three-month maternity leave, Karen found herself plugging away at work, fighting the distractions of part-time mothering. Sometimes she felt she wasn't doing a good job at either pursuit, trying to focus at her law office while her thoughts were back in Evanston, where Davi was in the hands of a benevolent nanny.

Karen couldn't wait each workday to rush home to Davi and Jon. But she knew that being a full-time mother, home all day long with Davi, wouldn't have worked either. She wanted to stay viable as a lawyer, keep up-to-speed with the world of estate-planning. Home all day with Davi as her only companion, she would have been restless, eager to do something else at least part of her day. Working part-time at Stein & Walter seemed to be the best possible work-life balance for her.

Karen and Jon's life together had a few ups and downs but overall was exceedingly happy, and Davi added to the happiness they shared. Settled in Evanston, Karen deliberately chose to avoid thinking about the small town of Walden, Wisconsin. Memories of that horrific town were best left forgotten. Karen chose, also, to never look back at her life in New York City. Life in Chicago was so much better.

Chapter 9

Stein & Walter.... With the files from Garrity & Costello no longer helpful, Karen realized she had to shift her focus to the nearly ten years she'd worked at Stein & Walter.

Because the firm's partners liked her work, they'd allowed her to continue working part-time while Davi was still small. Life had been good.

Too good, Karen reflected. Jon....

Karen found it painful to think about the earth-shattering day in August 2001 when she got the phone call that changed her life.

"Mrs. Smith?" a stranger's voice asked.

"Yes," Karen answered. Who was this caller? After marrying Jon, she occasionally called herself Karen Clark Smith. But no one who knew her called her "Mrs. Smith."

"It's about your husband, Mrs. Smith.... I think you'd better sit down."

The shocking news came fast. Jon had collapsed on the tennis court in Ackerman Park, playing his weekly lunchtime game with his partner, Hugh Goldberg. Hugh had administered CPR, then made sure Jon was rushed as fast as possible to Doctors Hospital. Now he was on life support, clinging to life while his heart struggled to keep him alive.

"Give me the phone," an angry voice interrupted. The voice softened when it came on the line. "Karen, it's Hugh. Come to the hospital right away. Jon...he might not make it."

By the time Karen arrived, it was too late. Jon was gone. Gone. Gone forever at 41.

It was sudden, unpredictable cardiac arrest, they told her. Something that no one saw coming.

Through the blur of decisions Karen had to make—the funeral, the burial, trying to explain to Davi what had happened—Karen couldn't help asking herself a million questions.

Had Jon known he had a heart problem? Hugh swore he didn't, but Karen couldn't be sure. She wracked her brain, dredging painfully through the past year or two, trying to discover whether he'd had any symptoms she'd missed.

There was that time they'd taken Davi to Great America. The temperature was in the 90s, and they were all sweating, but Jon had suddenly turned pale and shaky. He sat down on a bench until his color revived. "It's nothing," he assured Karen.

But had he been hiding something? To Karen? To himself? Trying to persuade both of them that he was okay, that there was nothing to worry about?

Karen remembered another time when Jon had been shaky, sweaty, his face pasty. They'd been at the outdoor Renaissance Faire just over the state line in Wisconsin. She'd insisted he sit down, out of the blazing sun, in a shady spot where he could cool off. By the time she brought him a cold drink, he'd recovered and looked perfectly fine.

But was that another instance of an incipient heart problem? A problem causing serious health concerns? Concerns Jon, as an M.D., should have paid attention to?

Dismissing them, was he hoping Karen would act, would insist he get a check-up to discover what was wrong? Like many physicians, had Jon ignored his own health problems, focusing instead on the problems of his patients?

Could Karen have done anything to keep Jon alive? Was there something she could have, should have done? She knew she'd be haunted by these questions for the rest of her life.

Chapter 10

Life without Jon. The man she met in Walden and fell in love with. The man she had married and made a life with in Chicago.

Losing Jon was painful, heart-wrenching, life-changing. It was so great a loss Karen couldn't find words to describe it. Most days she felt as though she were sleepwalking. She was numb, paralyzed, couldn't hear Jon's name without bursting into tears. It was a punch in the stomach every single day.

Life seemed so unfair. Her boundless bliss with Jon was suddenly supplanted by boundless grief. She tried Prozac and a grief-support group, but they barely made a dent in her grief, and she dropped them both.

Feeling responsible in part for Jon's death, for the gaping hole it had left in her life, Karen contemplated suicide. But she knew she couldn't do it. Because of Davi.

Davi now had only one parent. Without Karen, she would have no one.

Karen had no brothers or sisters, and her parents were both dead. She'd never had any sort of relationship with her father's second wife and didn't plan to create one.

A year or two after she married Jon, they got word that his parents had died in a collision caused by a drunk driver near their home in Sarasota. Jon had been shocked, losing both of his parents so suddenly, but he hadn't been in close touch with them, and he recovered quickly from the loss.

Karen remembered that Jon had once told her he had a sister in Minneapolis, but after Jon moved to Chicago, they'd drifted apart. When Davi was born and Jon called to give his sister the happy news, she announced that she'd volunteered for the Peace Corps and was about to take off for a small country in Africa. After that, Karen and Jon lost touch with her.

So Karen now felt very much alone. Alone and the only rock for Davi to hold on to. Luckily, Karen had made a few friends at work and in their Evanston neighborhood. She was grateful every day for Rosemary and Sid Carter, the next-door neighbors who'd befriended her from the beginning. They tried now to help Karen any way they could, but even their best efforts couldn't stem the tide of her grief.

At Stein & Walter, she'd felt close to two other women. She and Betsy Hilburn, a thirty-ish blonde partner in the health-care group, tried to lunch together once a week. Betsy would confide in Karen, relating her angst with some of the other partners.

Helen Penske, a dark-haired single woman in her late thirties, also hit it off with Karen, and they too tried to get together often. But to Karen's dismay, both women had left the firm during the late '90s, each for her own reasons.

Betsy regretfully moved to Dubai with her oil-and-gas connected husband. The firm gave her a big send-off as she departed for the Mideast and a prosperous though somewhat uncertain future.

Helen took a different path. Extremely aware that her biological clock was ticking, she decided to abandon her life as a lawyer who worked 60-hour weeks and instead open a small bakery on the Near North Side.

Karen wasn't surprised by Helen's decision. Her homemade blueberry muffins were legendary, and Karen always had difficulty resisting them in the 29th floor kitchen whenever Helen brought a platterful for her fellow lawyers. As Helen departed the firm, Karen hugged her, quietly wishing her all the happiness in the world. She didn't say it out loud, but she wished Helen what she wanted most--a delightful baby, like Davi, for her very own.

The demands of working at the firm, while Karen also tried to focus on her role as a mother, left little time to establish other close friendships at either work or home. Aside from her neighbors the Carters, and her lawyer-friends Betsy and Helen, Karen had built her life around Jon and Davi, and he'd built his around them. They hadn't felt a strong need to be close to anyone else.

But with Jon gone, Karen deeply regretted she hadn't formed enduring friendships with other women, women who might have been supportive now, when she needed them. Her few women friends outside the law firm, most of whom she'd met at casual get-togethers in her Evanston neighborhood, were all married. Happily married to healthy husbands. They were glad to meet Karen for lunch. But couples, she discovered, weren't eager to spend time with women who no longer had husbands of their own.

She often pondered exactly why. Were some of the husbands uneasy, sharing a meal with a woman whose husband had died so suddenly? Karen figured they found the prospect of early mortality in a relatively young man unsettling.

Did the wives feel threatened by a single woman who might lure a wife's husband into an illicit relationship? Karen had no interest in an alliance like that and scoffed at the idea. But she knew it probably lurked in the back of her friends' minds.

Even when she met her women friends for lunch, Karen wasn't always happy about the time they spent together. She often got tired of listening to their chit-chat, describing things they'd done with their husbands: "We" did this and "we" did that.

I hate the word "we," she decided.

But Karen was forced to admit she'd probably been guilty of doing the same thing when Jon was alive.

She knew she should try to create some new relationships, but who would she ally with? Other widows? Most widows were so much older than Karen. Women who could look back on 30, 40, even 50 years with their husbands. Karen was insanely jealous of them. She'd had only eight years with Jon.

No doubt she could track down some divorced women who'd prove friendly. But she wondered how many of them didn't have an ax to grind with men, who had men in their past who'd treasured them, adored them, as Jon had adored Karen.

She decided to make a real effort to meet other single women, either divorced or never married, as well as other widows. Surely she'd encounter some kindred souls. But she knew she wanted to steer away from embittered women who'd been abruptly and cruelly abandoned by their partners and were hostile to men as a result. She simply didn't share their hostility.

Karen's thoughts kept returning to Jon. She wanted so desperately to turn back time, to go back to the wonderful life she'd shared with him. Go back to the hint of symptoms that should have alerted her, alerted him, alerted his fellow physicians. Night after night, she cried herself to sleep, crying into her pillow to keep her sobs from disturbing Davi sleeping in the next room.

*   *   *

After four grief-filled months, Karen returned to part-time work at Stein & Walter, trying once again to balance that part of her life with the part she devoted to Davi. Davi seemed to be doing well, lovingly cared for by her longstanding nanny as well as Karen. At times, Davi seemed to miss the doting father who'd so mysteriously disappeared, but she was largely continuing the life she'd known before Jon died. Thankfully, Karen found she didn't need to worry a lot about Davi.

"Where's Daddy?" Davi had asked at the beginning. Karen doubted that, at four years old, Davi was able to grasp what had happened. She seemed reassured when Karen told her Daddy was sick and wouldn't be coming home for a while. But as Davi turned five, she asked more questions, and Karen finally decided to tell her the truth.

Davi was aware of the death of a beautiful dog, a golden retriever that had lived with the Carters next door. So Karen told her that Daddy had died, like the golden retriever, because he was very sick, and the doctors who took care of him weren't able to save his life.

"So Daddy's never coming home?" Davi asked. "Never?"

Karen nodded.

Davi burst into tears, burying her head in Karen's belly. "I miss Daddy...," she said.

Karen and Davi repeated this pattern several times before Davi seemed to gather up her five-year-old's strength and move on. But Karen knew Davi would continue to miss Jon's presence in her life.

Karen hoped she'd remember him forever.

Going back to work turned out to be therapeutic. Karen discovered that work provided a meaningful focus other than her grief. She plunged into her work, happy to reconnect with her clients, who'd missed seeing her.

After she'd been back at Stein & Walter for a few months, Karen was concentrating on a thorny estate-planning issue when she got an unexpected phone call. "Karen, it's Lisa Robbins. Your law-school classmate."

Karen searched her memory, trying to recall Lisa. After a minute, the smiling face of a tall, dishwater-blonde classmate slowly emerged. Lisa Robbins had been bright, friendly. She'd sat next to her in Torts. They'd become good friends, facing together the slings and arrows of student life at Harvard Law School.

"Lisa, it's great to hear from you...."

"I'll tell you why I'm calling. I went to our tenth class reunion in 2000, hoping to see you, but you didn't show up. I was just looking through the reunion Red Book, tracking down another practitioner in my field, and I came across the blurb you sent in. You're in Chicago, right? How are you doing?"

Karen swallowed hard. She hated this kind of call, a call forcing her to explain what had happened to her.

"Yes, I'm in Chicago, Lisa. And I couldn't make it to the reunion. I...I would have liked to see you again, but I was busy working part-time and raising my little one. Davi's just five now...."

"Right. I saw that in your blurb. Well, I'm going to be in Chicago on business next week. Would you like to get together while I'm there?"

Karen paused. The idea of seeing Lisa again was appealing, but could she go through the angst of explaining everything that had happened?

"Listen, Lisa, I should...," she began. "I...my husband died a little while ago, and I'm still reeling... I'm not sure I'm ready to meet with you. It might be...."

"Oh, jeez, Karen, I'm so sorry," Lisa interrupted. "I had no idea." Lisa paused. "But all the more reason to get together. I really want to see you. Maybe even help you get through whatever you're dealing with."

Karen finally relented and agreed to meet Lisa for lunch at the Corner Bakery on LaSalle Street. Once she saw Lisa's sympathetic face, she was glad she'd decided to see her again.

Karen poured out everything that had happened since law school. A condensed version to keep Lisa's eyes from glazing over. She asked Lisa a million questions, too, learning something about her exciting international-law practice in San Francisco.

Before saying goodbye, Lisa squeezed Karen's arm and told her she should think about moving to San Francisco. "I'll be in touch, Karen. I want you to think about leaving Chicago and coming out West," Lisa added. "Why stay here? You need to make a fresh start somewhere else. So let's talk. I'll help you work something out."

Karen gave Lisa a half-hearted smile and nodded. "Maybe....," she said. Not really meaning it.

Chapter 11

Karen landed in San Francisco two years after she'd first heard from Lisa Robbins. Lisa's unfailing encouragement to move had lodged in her brain from the beginning. Karen remembered helping Lisa get through a bad break-up during law school, and Lisa now seemed eager to help Karen in return.

"Karen," Lisa would say in one of her frequent phone calls, "you need to make a fresh start. San Francisco IS that fresh start. You'll love living here. The weather, the people, the natural beauty all around us...it'll be a brand new life for you. Your daughter, too."

Karen hesitated at first, but Lisa kept calling, kept sending one email message after another, urging Karen to leave Chicago, leave her life there behind, and start a new life in San Francisco.

Karen had to admit she wasn't terribly happy on her own in Chicago. She'd tried to make a life for herself without Jon, and she'd made a few new friends. But most of the lawyers at Stein & Walter were too focused on boosting their own careers to spend much time with their part-time colleague. Karen even suspected that some of the firm's lawyers resented her part-time status, which management had kindly allowed her to continue. She knew these other lawyers had made pleas to work part-time, but they'd been largely unsuccessful. Karen often got the vibe that she shouldn't be able to do what they couldn't.

Sadly, she still didn't have a host of single friends to fall back on. She'd tried befriending some of the new hires at the firm, but they were so stressed by the volume of work they were expected to handle that they usually brushed off her attempts to form any kind of social bond.

She did get together now and then with Helen Penske, her former colleague at the firm. Whenever Karen could get there, they would meet up at Helen's thriving Near North Side bakery, Muffins Forever, a venue now celebrated by the local media. And the Carters introduced her to a new single neighbor on their block, Mary Ann McRae. The two women went to the movies and dinner in downtown Evanston a couple of times before drifting apart.

Karen kept trying to make the most of her single life in Chicago. One night she went to the symphony by herself, relishing the opportunity to hear one of the world's great orchestras playing pieces by her favorite composers, Mozart and Beethoven. But glancing at all the couples surrounding her, she felt lonely and unhappy. Karen concluded that leaving Davi with a sitter while she tried to immerse herself in beautiful music, absent someone like Jon beside her, was an expensive mistake. *I'd rather be home alone with Davi.*

One Saturday, Karen ran into Rosemary Carter. "How are you doing, Karen?" Rosemary asked, empathy lighting up her beautiful brown eyes. After some chit-chat, Rosemary asked whether Karen felt secure, alone with a small child in her house.

"I...I guess so," Karen said. In truth, she often felt nervous, especially after Davi went to sleep and Karen became highly aware of how alone she was, how vulnerable she would be to intruders.

"Did you ever try to learn any kind of self-defense?" Rosemary asked.

"No...not really," Karen said, remembering how she'd avoided taking any self-defense classes offered during her college years at Princeton, preferring to focus on her academic studies instead.

"Maybe you'd like to take up tae kwon do with me," Rosemary suggested. "I go to classes at a small place just off Central Street on Wednesday nights. It gives me a really good feeling, knowing I can protect myself if I ever need to."

"But I can't leave Davi...."

"Sid would be happy to watch her while we go to class together. Why don't you come with me next Wednesday and see how you like it?"

Karen was dubious, but she impulsively decided to attend Rosemary's class. Much to her surprise, she liked the teacher and the positive feeling she got, almost immediately, from his instruction. Continuing with the classes each week, she began to feel stronger and much more confident about her ability to protect herself. She knew it was unlikely she could fend off a determined intruder, but she was at least in better shape to deal with any threat like that. Happily, she was no longer as fearful of being alone in her house as she'd been.

Karen's primary focus hadn't changed. She was still trying to keep her head above water at the law firm while she made every effort to help Davi adjust to having one parent. Dealing with Chicago weather, especially during the long, gray, snow-filled winters, made things even tougher. The phone calls from Lisa Robbins continued, and a move to San Francisco more and more seemed like a plausible alternative.

Karen finally flew to San Francisco to check out the possible contours of her life there. Davi, at nearly seven, was reluctant to see her leave, and Karen didn't want to disrupt Davi's life any more than necessary. But she needed to visit San Francisco before she could make any sort of rational decision.

"I'll miss you so much, Mommy," Davi said.

"I'll only be gone a few days," Karen said. "I need to visit my friend Lisa."

Davi thought about it, finally deciding that Karen's trip would be a good idea. "Go ahead, Mommy," she said. "I'll be fine. Just remember to call me every morning and every night."

Karen assured Davi that she would and took off the next day for San Francisco, leaving Davi with the Carters, who were happy to have her cheerful company. "Davi's great fun," Rosemary said, her cocoa-brown skin and short-cropped Afro gleaming under the light from the Carters' kitchen ceiling. "Sid and I will love having her stay here."

Lisa met Karen at SFO and enthusiastically drove her around the Bay Area, focusing on the neighborhoods in San Francisco where Karen might want to settle. It was Karen's first trip to the area, and it was love at first sight. She responded immediately to the natural beauty surrounding the city, the Golden Gate Bridge glinting in the sun, the striking Victorian houses set on the city's many hills, the smaller pastel houses that dotted the neighborhoods, the charming boutiques on Union Street.

The first priority was finding a place to live. Karen was attracted to the area encompassing Pacific Heights and Cow Hollow, and scanning

Craig's List, discovered an array of apartments that seemed suitable for her and Davi.

"But I need to find a job first, Lisa," she explained. How could she make a giant leap like this, moving to a new location without a job?

"I've got plenty of contacts, Karen. You want to stay with estate-planning?"

Karen nodded.

"Let me put you in touch with a couple of firms that do that kind of work. You'll find a place pretty fast," Lisa assured her.

The job market for lawyers was thriving that year, and after a couple of brief interviews, one small firm, Franklin & Cooper, was ready to hire Karen even before she passed the California bar exam.

"We'll give you a temporary slot, Karen. Just till you manage to get settled and take the California bar," Abby Plummer told her. "We've been inundated with work lately. A lot of real-estate and estate-planning clients. We need someone like you right now. With your background and experience, you can help us out without being a member of the bar...for a while at least. You look like a pretty safe bet," Abby smiled.

Karen returned to Chicago, arriving at O'Hare in the midst of an April blizzard. But even confronting the snow-caused delays at O'Hare didn't make her decision an easy one. She still wasn't certain that moving was the right thing to do. But she was inching closer and closer. She was beginning to think she'd take a chance on it.

I can always come back here, she told herself. *I won't burn all my bridges, just try life in San Francisco and see how it goes.*

49

Extracting herself from her house in Evanston and her job at Stein & Walter was a challenge. But with a hot housing market on the North Shore, her small home near Evanston's Central Street sold fast, rewarding Karen with much more than she and Jon had paid for it. Thankfully, they hadn't accumulated a lot of stuff, and a local moving company assured her it could easily pack it all up and ship it to California. She also decided to jettison the car she'd needed for her life in Evanston but wouldn't need in San Francisco, where she hoped to get around on public transportation, at least at first.

Leaving the law firm was more complicated. Her clients, who relied on her for comforting advice, were hard to abandon. They weren't happy when she announced she was leaving the firm and moving to California. "But Karen," they told her, "we want you to stay. Please don't pull up stakes and leave us."

But Karen was able to reassure them, demonstrate how the shift to her colleague Drew Lewis would work smoothly, and all would be well. At the end, the firm gave a low-key farewell party for her at the Middle Eastern restaurant where Karen and Jon had loved to feast on highly marinated shish-kebab. She fought back tears as she looked around at her colleagues, toasting her with a glass of chardonnay, wishing her well.

I didn't want it to end like this, she thought. We should have been toasting a meritorious victory in court, an estate well settled, someone's new baby. Not my sudden departure from the firm, my sudden departure from this life. Jon should have been here....

Explaining the move to Davi took a while. Davi had matured into a bright and socially adept seven-year-old. She'd developed a circle of friends, other second-graders who claimed they'd miss her, even though Karen suspected that once Davi moved, almost all of them would forget her.

But Davi wanted, above all, to be with Karen. Karen knew that Davi still missed Jon, her charming and devoted Daddy. But in his absence, Davi wanted to cling to Karen and make Karen happy. And so she smiled and cheerfully agreed to pack up her treasures and leave Evanston for San Francisco.

Chapter 12

Settled in a sun-drenched apartment in San Francisco by the summer of 2004, Karen and Davi fell into a comfortable pattern in their new home. Karen had chosen her apartment carefully. As carefully as she could during three frantic days of apartment-hunting with Lisa Robbins.

She chose a location on the border between Pacific Heights and Cow Hollow, a charming neighborhood that featured quiet streets and tall trees, mostly California sycamores, a tree she'd never seen in the eastern part of the country. Close-by apartment buildings included stunning examples of Art Deco structures with beautiful terra cotta facades and ornate lobbies whose décor probably dated from the 1930s.

With the substantial pile of cash she got for selling her house in Evanston, Karen rented a large two-bedroom apartment featuring high ceilings and a south-facing bay window in the living room. It was bright and spacious, and Karen viewed it as a good transition for herself and Davi as they made a new life for themselves in San Francisco.

She'd missed renting a place with a view of the Bay by a split-second. As she'd entered the other building to sign the lease, she heard a man saying "I'll take it." So she'd have no view of the Bay. But she was happy with her sunny view of the beautiful Victorian houses across the street and the tall sycamores just outside her window.

Karen's new location suited her well. For one thing, it made commuting downtown easy, with four different bus routes that could take her near her office. She knew they'd also serve as a good way to get to the downtown museums, symphony hall, and the opera house.

And Karen was happily able to enroll Davi in a highly regarded elementary school, Sheraton School, only a few blocks away. She and Davi could walk there together every school-day morning, and Karen planned to line up a babysitter who could pick up Davi after school. Her building's friendly manager lived on her floor and cheerfully helped her get settled in her new apartment. Living in what appeared to be a tranquil low-crime area was reassuring as well.

While Karen got underway at her law firm, she registered her daughter in some summer programs in the city, and Davi immediately made fast friends among her new companions. She was able to stay late at these programs, created for working parents, until Karen could pick her up after work. When the programs ended, and school hadn't yet begun, Karen was able to arrange one play date after another with Davi's new friends.

From the outset, Karen relished her work at the small firm of Franklin & Cooper, a firm that represented a wide range of small businesses and individuals. Karen's work focused almost exclusively on estate-planning, the same kind of thing she'd been doing in Chicago. Until she could take the California bar exam, Karen concentrated on learning the ins and outs of California trusts and estates law, assisting Abby and the other partners with the kind of research she was highly skilled at.

Although her new life seemed to be falling into place, there were still brief moments when Karen questioned her decision to move to San

Francisco. Trying to develop a rapport with new people in a new city sometimes seemed an unsurmountable challenge.

Has my decision to move been a mistake? Assaulted by disturbing thoughts like that, Karen would straighten her shoulders, sit all the way back in her black leather desk chair, and resolve to look forward, not back.

That was what her move to San Francisco was all about, wasn't it? It was the fresh start she'd wanted, the fresh start that meant a whole new life for her and Davi. And so far, she had to admit that she loved life in San Francisco.

She relished the vibrant pace of the city, much like that in Chicago, but here it was accompanied by great weather, charming neighborhoods, and the stunning natural backdrops that surrounded the city.

Karen and Davi spent their weekends exploring the city. One Saturday they walked to Chestnut Street, eating lunch at The Grove and plunging into the wealth of offerings at the wonderful bookstore across the street. Davi selected two colorful storybooks while Karen perused the abundance of books devoted to San Francisco and nearby sites outside the city. Karen bought a thick guidebook, resolving to take Davi to Muir Woods, a beautiful redwoods forest just north of the city, lauded by every guidebook she skimmed.

The next Saturday, Karen and Davi took the Van Ness bus to Tommy's Joynt for an early dinner. Karen had been wanting to try the food at Tommy's, another guidebook favorite, located at Van Ness and Geary. She and Davi stood in line, ordered turkey sandwiches from the friendly man behind the counter, and ate in their own private booth, surrounded by other happy eaters. The bar featured a vast number of beers, imported and domestic, but Karen forwent those in favor of soft drinks for both her and Davi.

"They serve buffalo meat here, Mommy," a wide-eyed Davi remarked when she read the menu. "Can we come back and order that sometime?"

"We'll see," Karen said, not quite sure that was a good idea. She wanted to research it first.

On another Saturday, the two headed for Fillmore Street, where they met up with Abby Plummer for lunch at another outpost of The Grove. Together, the three of them pored over the book selection at another great bookstore, just a block or two away from The Grove. Abby finally drove off in her Camry, returning home to the East Bay, while Karen bought two more storybooks for Davi and a brand-new thriller for herself, plus some essentials at Walgreens, before they made their way home on foot.

Davi loved to be outdoors, so they often trekked to the two public parks in their neighborhood, Alta Plaza and Lafayette, whose sunny and colorful playgrounds beckoned. Karen sat back on a park bench and happily watched Davi swing on the swings and teeter on the teeter-totter, knowing she could play there year-round, even when the winter months arrived.

As summer turned to fall, Karen hoped to set out on excursions to other parts of the city. She wanted to explore Chinatown and a whole host of other sights described in her new guidebook. But most of these excursions would have to wait. Davi had started third grade at Sheraton

School, and she liked staying close to home, working on her homework, or going to the park with Karen on the weekends.

Karen's attempts to reconnect with Lisa Robbins worked out well at first. They had lunch together a few times downtown, and one night Karen asked her babysitter to stay with Davi so she and Lisa could enjoy dinner at Kuleto's, followed by the latest offering at a theater on Geary Street. But Karen soon discovered that Lisa's high-pressure law practice consumed a huge amount of time, sometimes making it tough for them to get together.

One sunny Saturday, Lisa somehow found time to pick up both Karen and Davi and drive them around the city, just as she'd driven Karen around months before. Going through Golden Gate Park, they luckily found a parking spot just across from a remarkable Victorian glass and wooden structure, the Conservatory of Flowers, and went inside to immerse themselves in the abundant greenery and flowers. Davi especially liked some of the exotic succulents she'd never seen before.

Lisa then guided them to the park's nearly 100-year-old carousel, where Davi enthusiastically mounted one of the colorful horses and begged to stay on for ride after ride. The threesome finished the afternoon by sampling Burmese food on Clement Street, not far from another busy bookstore, and Karen vowed to return to the park and to Clement Street as soon as she could.

After Karen had been in San Francisco for several months, she and Lisa met for lunch at Lisa's favorite restaurant on Belden Place, Café Bastille, and Lisa dropped a bomb. "The firm's moving me to Hong

Kong," she said. Lisa looked down, fixing her eyes on the tablecloth covering the space between them, unable to look directly at Karen.

Karen was in truth shocked to learn that Lisa, the friend who'd encouraged her to pull up stakes in Chicago and move to San Francisco, would be leaving the city. Her heart sank at the prospect of Lisa's departure. "When?" she asked.

"Next month. It's been in the works for a while, but nothing definitive happened until this week," Lisa said, looking up at Karen. "I'm really sorry to be abandoning you. I was looking forward to spending lots of time with you...helping you get settled, going on hikes together...."

Karen nodded, mute, unable to be happy for her friend. Lisa would be setting out on an exciting adventure. But one that left Karen in the lurch.

"Don't worry about it, Lisa," she finally blurted out. "If you're happy about it, I'm happy for you. You'll be coming back here now and then, won't you?"

"Oh, sure. I'll need to update my partners in person once in a while. So we'll stay in touch and get together whenever we can," Lisa concluded with a half-hearted attempt at a smile.

Karen attempted a smile as well, but her heart wasn't in it. Her hopes for a close bond with Lisa had suddenly vanished. She'd go on trying to look forward, to look ahead to good times in San Francisco, but it now seemed so much harder.

Lisa interrupted Karen's reverie. "Hey, I have a great idea for you," she said brightly. "You could join a fitness club. Like the one I go to on

Market Street. It's a terrific way to meet people. There are lots of new transplants like you."

Karen wondered how she could ever find time to patronize a fitness club. She barely had time to shepherd Davi to school, get herself to work, make dinner almost every night, and monitor her finances. She sometimes thought about resuming classes in tae kwon do at a school in the area, but with all the demands on her time, she barely had a spare moment to read the morning *Chronicle* or glance at the thriller she'd just bought.

Lisa paused. She seemed to sense how unrealistic the idea of a fitness club was for Karen. But a minute later, she brightened again. "Wait. Here's another idea. You and I met at Harvard, and that's the connection between us, isn't it?"

Karen nodded.

"It just occurred to me," Lisa went on, "you'd probably like meeting some of the other Harvard grads who live here. Have you thought about joining the local Harvard Club?"

Karen shook her head. She hadn't even known there was a Harvard Club in San Francisco.

"It's a pretty active group," Lisa added. "There's a whole bunch of events every week or two, and you can meet other Harvard alums that way. I've gone to a couple of events myself, and they were kind of fun...."

Karen had never joined any alumni clubs, never joined any clubs like that anywhere. There'd never been enough time, and she'd never felt the need to meet people that way. But she had to admit she often felt lonely. And Lisa's departure would leave her feeling even lonelier.

She was inclined to dismiss the idea, but she'd think about it. Maybe check to see whether the Harvard Club had some activities she'd enjoy. It was definitely something to think about.

Chapter 13

Joining the Harvard Club turned out to be an excellent idea. Karen paid the small membership fee, then pushed herself to attend a couple of events. Davi grumbled a bit when Karen would take off for an evening event. "Don't go!" she'd pout. "I want you to stay home!"

Karen would assure her that she wouldn't be away very long. Luckily, Davi was usually happy to stay home with her babysitter, Juanita. Once Davi and Juanita huddled together over a jigsaw puzzle or a TV sitcom, Karen could leave without feeling terribly guilty.

The alums she met at these events were, for the most part, friendly and interesting. Many seemed genuinely happy to meet her, and when they learned she was a recent transplant to San Francisco, they were eager to learn more about her decision to move to their city.

"Where did you move from?" was a common question. When Karen replied "Chicago," she often got an unexpected response: "I've heard Chicago is a great city.... Why did you move *here*?"

Karen didn't want to downgrade Chicago—it had been a good place to live, at least while Jon was alive—but she was astonished to come across San Franciscans who questioned her decision to move. Weren't they thrilled to be living in the beautiful and exciting city she now called home? Had they lost sight of how remarkable their lives in San Francisco really were? They clearly had no idea how many envious comments Karen heard from people in Chicago when they learned about her move.

"Oh, you're so lucky!" her favorite supermarket cashier told Karen when she revealed her plans. "I wish I could move there!" Karen got the same reaction from others, over and over again. Lana—one of the paralegals at Stein & Walter—nearly drooled with envy when she heard Karen was moving to San Francisco.

The people she met in San Francisco who questioned her move? Karen chalked up their attitude to complacency, to a failure to realize how unpleasant life elsewhere could be.

Karen would rush to answer politely, "Yes, Chicago's a great city, but...after my husband died, I didn't want to stay there. I wanted to make a fresh start." People nodded, seeming to understand. But Karen doubted that they really understood how lonely her life in Chicago had become after Jon died and how much she treasured her new life in San Francisco.

At one event, the annual Harvard Club evening at the city's opera, Karen relished plunging into the maelstrom of excited opera-goers as she entered the imposing marble-clad Opera House on Van Ness Avenue. The club held a pre-opera wine reception for members, featuring the director of the San Francisco Opera. He boastfully maintained that his opera company was the second largest in the country, even though San Francisco's population paled in comparison to that in cities like Chicago and L.A.

While alums cheered the director's boasts, Karen looked around, wondering whether any of them looked like people she'd want to know. After the director finished speaking and the crowd began to head for their seats, Karen noticed a couple of likely candidates. Two relatively good-looking men in their 40s, or maybe their 50s—it was hard to tell-- were gulping down the last of their wine.

Karen smiled in their direction, wondering whether they'd notice her. The taller man looked interested. He leaned over and said something to his companion, who seemed reluctant to move. Finally the taller man won the argument, and they both made their way to where she was standing.

"Hi," Karen said tentatively, trying to judge whether they would postpone getting to their seats long enough to talk to her.

"Hi there," the taller one said, perusing her with interest. "You are...?"

"Karen Clark. And you are?"

"Cameron Harper. My friends call me Cam."

Piercing blue eyes peered at her beneath neatly groomed eyebrows. An equally well-groomed salt-and-pepper beard completed his appearance. Turning to the other man, he added, "This is Ken Pryce. Pryce spelled with a 'y.'"

Ken had thinning gray hair and sharp features in a narrow face. "We've known each other since our days at Harvard, right, Ken?" Cam said.

Ken nodded, clearly uninterested in pursuing a conversation with Karen. "I'm going to find my seat," he said brusquely, turning and walking toward an entrance to the auditorium.

"I guess I'd better go as well," Cam said. "But Karen...I'd really like to talk to you sometime. How can I get in touch with you?"

"I'm working at Franklin & Cooper. A law firm on Market Street," Karen said.

Cam nodded approvingly. "What's your specialty?" he asked.

"Estate-planning," she replied. "You know, writing wills and trusts. That kind of thing."

Cam nodded again, smiling broadly this time. "I could probably use a new will," he laughed. "Maybe we can meet for lunch sometime. I might become a client of yours."

"That sounds great," Karen said, wondering whether Cam Harper would actually contact her.

The warning bell sounded, and those who were still there moved toward the doors.

"We'd better go in now, Karen. It's been lovely to meet you," Cam said with a warm smile. "I'll be in touch." Cam turned and took off.

Karen looked around her. Everyone else had left the reception. Karen hastily joined them, preparing to be delighted by "The Marriage of Figaro" for the third time in her life. Or was it the fourth?

Chapter 14

Soon after her night at the opera, Karen exited the 41 bus and entered her apartment building one evening after work. She was heading for her mailbox when she noticed a neighbor fussing over his.

"Damn!" he said loudly. As Karen approached, he turned toward her. "Oh, sorry, little lady. I'm having a terrible time with my key today." The older man looked about 80 or 85, his face covered with deep furrows.

Years of sun damage, Karen figured. Like so many older Californians, he'd probably spent years soaking up the sun, totally unprotected from its dangerous rays. The result was a plethora of wrinkles, not to mention the likelihood of skin cancer of one sort or another.

The man's bald pate gleamed under the overhead light illuminating the brass mailboxes. A crusty area on his scalp looked as though it could already be skin cancer.

"Can I help you?" Karen offered.

"It's this key. Maybe your young hands can get it to turn. My old ones can't," he said with a frown.

"Let me try." Karen smiled. At 40, she relished being called "young." She tried moving the key in the lock, and presto! The mailbox opened.

"Hey," the man said. "That's just great. Thanks...uh.... I don't know your name...."

"Karen. Karen Clark."

"Well, thanks, Karen Clark," he said. His frown had vanished, replaced by a smile. "Would you like to come up to my apartment for a cup of coffee? I owe you something for helping me with my mail," he added, pulling a stack of letters and junk mail out of his mailbox.

Karen thought she saw a batch of solicitation envelopes, much like the ones she got every day. His were different, though. They seemed to focus exclusively on pictures of starving children and woeful-looking dogs.

Karen had assumed that the deluge of pleas for money would become a trickle when she moved to a new address, but she was wrong. Somehow all those senders tracked her down, assaulting her mailbox with just as many pleas as she'd received in Evanston. Some still had Jon's name on the envelope. How did all those acquisitive entities find her at her new address? Was the U.S. Postal Service in on it?

"Well, missy, what do you say?" Karen's bald neighbor was waiting for a reply.

"Oh, thank you very much, but I was happy to help, Mr. .... What's your name, sir?"

"Whitlock. Gordon Whitlock."

"Well, thanks for the invitation, but I really must get upstairs, Mr. Whitlock. My daughter is waiting for me to have dinner with her." Karen couldn't wait to see Davi again and spend the evening with her, hearing about her day at school, helping her with her homework.

"Daughter? Is she the cute little girl I've seen around here lately?" A simpering grin had crept onto his face.

"Yes, yes, she probably is, Mr. Whitlock. And now I really must run."

"Please, it's Gordon. And I hope you'll take me up on my offer of coffee sometime. You, and your cute little daughter, too."

Karen nodded, smiling, grabbing her own mail, making a bee-line for the elevator. Hoping Gordon Whitlock wouldn't move fast enough to get to the elevator, possibly delaying her. She wanted to get upstairs to Davi as fast as she could.

But she needn't have worried. Gordon had dropped a few pieces of his mail, mostly envelopes covered with images of destitute children, and he was busy picking them up.

"Bye," Karen called out as she entered the elevator. She was eager to get to know her neighbors, including Gordon. But she was more interested in some of the others she'd seen around the building. Especially that good-looking guy who lived on the fourth floor. She was hoping to meet him next.

Chapter 15

A month after Davi's abduction, Greg Chan called Karen at her office one morning. "No new leads, Karen," he reported. "Sorry."

Karen pictured Greg's handsome face looking apologetic as he passed along the disappointing news. "Well, thanks for following up, Greg. I appreciate it. Let me know if you hear anything. Anything at all."

Karen hung up, feeling dispirited. Still shaken by what had happened, she continued every day to search her brain for clues. What had led to Davi's abduction? And the note pinned to her shirt?

Now that Garrity & Costello's dusty files had proved to be unhelpful, Karen knew she had to focus on her time at Stein & Walter. Maybe an explanation was somewhere in the contacts she'd made there.

There was one complication. Law firms like Stein & Walter no longer had a host of "secretaries" like Melissa Cohen, her devoted secretary at Garrity & Costello in New York. For the most part, the firms now employed "assistants" who worked for a large number of lawyers, never developing the kind of close connection, even comradeship, Karen had forged with Melissa. They were all part of the loosely-termed "support staff."

Karen was now forced to consider who she could call upon at Stein & Walter for help. Was there anyone at the firm who could get her the files she needed to review?

Even though Karen had left the firm little more than a year earlier, she couldn't think of anyone who was likely to come to her aid. After Davi was born, Karen had been preoccupied with trying to balance her time spent working at the firm with time devoted to Davi and her life with Jon. Later, after Jon died, she was constantly striving to keep her head above water, putting in time at the firm while she tried to make a life without Jon for herself and Davi. The friends she'd made early on had gone on to other places. By the time Karen left the firm, she had very few close relationships she could count on.

She first tried calling Drew Lewis, the colleague at Stein & Walter who'd taken on most of her clients. But his voicemail message said he was on an extended vacation. No helpful support would come from that quarter.

Who else could she call upon? Finally she remembered the name of a young paralegal, Lana Dumbarton, who'd amiably worked with her once or twice. But when she tried to track Lana down via the Stein & Walter website, Karen discovered that the paralegal was no longer at the firm. She vaguely recalled Lana's envy when she learned about Karen's move to San Francisco. Had Lana had left Chicago and made a similar move of her own?

Karen tried to come up with another name. Wasn't there a kindly assistant named Jane? Jane what? Jane Hopper or Hooper or...? Karen searched for a name like that on the firm's website and found a phone number for Jane Hooper. Her hands shaking, she picked up her office phone and tried calling.

"Stein & Walter, Jane Hooper speaking," a cheerful voice said. Karen sighed with relief, picturing the 40ish dark-haired woman she remembered.

"Jane, Jane...this is Karen Clark. I worked as a lawyer at Stein & Walter.... I did mainly estate-planning, but...."

"Oh, yes, I remember you," Jane said brightly. "Didn't you move somewhere out West? A year or two ago?"

"Yes, yes, that's right," Karen said quickly, hoping Jane would stay on the line. "I moved to San Francisco about a year ago. And now I'm wondering whether you can help me with something...."

"Help you? Sorry, but I'm swamped, Karen. I have about four partners demanding stuff from me right now. I really don't have a minute to help...."

"Just listen, please, Jane. I'd like to get copies of some files--for cases I handled at the firm. It's extremely..."

"Karen, I'm sorry," Jane interrupted. "There's no way I can help you. For one thing, we're in chaos here. We've lost some of our partners, and everyone's scrambling to keep our clients happy. I couldn't begin to help you."

"But..."

"Even if I had time to help you, I couldn't send you your old files. We don't give our former lawyers their files unless a client directs us to. That's firm policy. I guess you didn't know."

Jane abruptly hung up, leaving Karen in a state of silent shock.

Where can I turn now?

Chapter 16

Karen worried incessantly about her daughter, but Davi was proving to be resilient. She was doing well under Vera Haglund's care, seeing the therapist only twice a week now, and Vera's reports to Karen were encouraging.

Although Vera had initially suggested that Davi transfer to a new school, a new environment, Karen's instincts told her otherwise. And her instincts were right. Back at Sheraton School, surrounded by friends and teachers from the previous year, Davi seemed to be thriving. At home, she loved to curl up with one of her storybooks in a living room chair next to the bay window, her blonde curls gleaming in the sun.

At Lafayette Park one sunny Sunday, Karen was watching Davi running and jumping in the playground with another young girl when Karen noticed a scruffy-looking man whose gaze seemed to be fixated on the two girls. Was he the other girl's father? Or was he merely some random guy who'd perched on a park bench to soak up the sun? Or something else entirely? It was hard to tell.

Karen didn't want to prejudge the man on the basis of his rather sketchy appearance. She figured he might even be an affluent type who simply chose to "dress down" on his Sunday off from work as, say, the CEO at a Silicon Valley startup. But the man's gaze never left blonde-haired Davi, even when her dark-haired friend took off to play with another child.

The man's fixed gaze disturbed Karen. She thought she might have seen the same man at the park once before, and he'd disturbed her equanimity then, too. Finally, Karen decided to take matters into her own hands and approached Davi, insisting on removing her from the playground despite Davi's strong opposition. "But Mom," Davi protested, "I'm having so much fun!"

"Sorry, sweetie, but we have to leave now," Karen insisted, dragging Davi away from her beloved playground, offering a visit to a nearby frozen yogurt shop instead.

Karen liked escorting Davi to a lot of different places near their home. She left work early one day and picked up Davi at school. They walked together to Polk Street, where they browsed the gift items and used books at a favorite bookstore and indulged in greasy burgers at Polker's before returning home. Another time, they set out to find the "Mrs. Doubtfire" house at Broadway and Steiner. Davi had just watched the DVD of the Robin Williams classic and wanted to see the house for herself. It was a challenging walk from their apartment, but they found the house and celebrated with dinner at nearby Rose's Café. And a new-found favorite for dinner was Perry's on Union Street, a bit closer to home.

Although Karen was relieved that Davi was doing well, she couldn't help worrying, not only about Davi's recovery but about her own safety as well. "You're next, Karen...." It was impossible to drum that message out of her head. She woke every morning wondering just what it meant. And whether it could lead, would lead, to her own abduction.

She tried to hide her fears from Davi, an effort that seemed to be succeeding. The effort suppressed the fears in her own mind as well. But each morning, waking up alone in the queen-sized bed she'd shared with Jon and perhaps unwisely moved to San Francisco, the phrase came back to haunt her.

Greg Chan finally got back to her again. The investigation was moving slowly and he had little news to report, but he did convey some information. About Diana Street.

"It's a dead end, Karen," he told her in a phone call one afternoon.

"A dead end?"

"Not literally. What I mean is our house-to-house search hasn't turned up anything. The guys checked all fifteen houses. They had to go back two or three times before they could talk to all of the homeowners. We can probably let you see a list of their names if you think they might mean something to you."

Karen doubted whether she knew anyone living in the Bayview. She'd hardly met anyone outside her law firm. A few people, like Gordon Whitlock, in her apartment building, a couple of members of the Harvard Club, and a mother or two at Davi's school. But it was probably a waste of time to look at the list of the homeowners on Diana Street.

"No, don't bother," she told Greg.

"Eventually they all let us into their houses, let us search for a brown sofa, anything else that might seem suspicious, but everything looked okay. No scary types living there, no brown sofas, nothing suspicious or unusual."

Karen's heart sank. Diana Street...it had offered up the hope of some sort of answer to what had happened to Davi. To what might happen to Karen herself.

"Well, thanks, Greg. Thanks for having your guys check out all those houses. I wish you'd found something, but..."

"So do I, Karen. I was hoping that would happen. I'm sorry it didn't."

"So...," Karen started to say. She paused, not sure what else to say.

"I'll let you know if I come up with something new, Karen. In the meantime, try not to worry. Things seem to have settled down. I wouldn't worry too much about it."

Easy for you to say, Karen thought. She lived with constant worry, but she couldn't expect Greg Chan to see things the same way.

"How's your daughter doing, by the way?" Greg asked.

"Pretty well," Karen said. "Surprisingly well."

"Yeah, kids are resilient. I'm glad she's okay."

"Thanks."

"Oh, before I forget...," Greg added hastily. "Do you know any of your neighbors?"

"A few...."

"Just thought I'd tell you we've been looking into an older man in your building. He tried to volunteer at a school in the city, but the principal wasn't sure about letting him do it. She asked us to check him out."

Karen panicked. Who was it? Gordon Whitlock, with his apparent fondness for random children? Or someone else?

"Can you tell me his name?" she asked.

"I can't say any more at this point," Greg said. "But don't worry about it right now," he added. "It may amount to nothing. Just keep your eyes open, and let me know about anyone who strikes you as a little off."

Karen hung up, a fog of depression descending on her. This news about someone in her building was unsettling. Could there be someone living virtually next door who preyed on children? Did he see Davi around the building and decide to go after her? It seemed unlikely, but...maybe she should tell Greg about Gordon Whitlock.

Also troubling was the fact that Diana Street hadn't led to any breakthroughs. Was she missing something else that might?

She suddenly realized that the name "Diana" had another meaning. "Diana." Wasn't that the name of a Roman goddess? The goddess of the hunt?

She remembered seeing images of the goddess Diana at the Metropolitan Museum of Art when she lived in New York and was able to shunt aside her pile of work for a few hours and visit the museum. One was a painting of a full-figured Diana by a sixteenth-century Italian painter. Karen and her then-boyfriend Jason had paused in front of it for a long time, admiring her classic beauty. On another trip to the Met, this time by herself one Saturday morning, Karen came across Saint-Gaudens's sculpture in the American wing. It was a very different take on Diana--a slim bronze figure, poised on tiptoe, about to shoot one of her arrows. Karen had fallen in love with it.

Now Karen had lots of questions. Did the goddess Diana inspire the madman who'd grabbed Davi outside the 7-Eleven? More importantly, how did Davi become aware of the connection?

Davi remembered "Red Diana." Why?

Was it possible that the abductor had a reproduction of the Saint-Gaudens sculpture in the room where Davi was trapped? Maybe it was identified somehow as a depiction of Diana. Maybe a red scarf was wrapped around it. Or maybe the madman had a framed reproduction of the Italian painting, the name "Diana" appearing somewhere on the frame. But how would that have led Davi to come up with "Red Diana"?

Karen wanted to ferret out the answers to her questions, but how? And when? She'd have to focus on those questions another time. She needed to get some of her work done first.

In truth, Karen's days at work were mercifully busy. She signed up for a course to prepare for the California bar exam, adding something else to plug into her daily schedule in another month or two. And every day that passed without another frightening phone call, or another scary message constructed from newspaper headlines, was a good one.

*   *   *

When her office phone rang one morning, she didn't recognize the caller-ID name: B Hertz. Hertz? The rental car company? Why would Hertz be calling her? She hadn't rented a car from Hertz in years.

Karen assumed it was an annoying solicitation or a wrong number. But she decided to answer, hoping to dispose of the call right away instead of having it go to voicemail.

"Karen?" The voice at the other end didn't sound like a robotic solicitation voice. More like a very warm and friendly one.

"Karen, it's Brad. Brad Hertz. Remember me?"

"Brad?" Karen was startled to hear Brad's name again. Was it the Brad she knew in law school?

"Your law-school classmate." Brad's tone was now somewhat more reserved. "Is this Karen Clark?"

"Yes, yes. It's Karen Clark. Brad...I'm sorry. I was...I was...."

"That's okay. I'm just glad I reached you. Lisa Robbins told me you were in San Francisco, and I thought I'd call, see if we could get together while I'm in town...."

In her mind's eye, Karen summoned up a picture of Brad Hertz. Bright, good-looking, sexy. She'd had an enormous crush on him. But after a few dates during law school, they'd drifted apart and gone their own ways after graduation. Karen had gone off to work on Wall Street at Garrity & Costello, while Brad, like Lisa Robbins, had pursued a career in international law. Karen later noticed in one of the reunion Red Books that he was married and living in D.C.

"I'm in town for a couple of days," Brad was saying. "Would you like to get together for lunch?"

"Sure, sure," Karen said. "When?"

"My meeting just got cancelled. Are you free today?"

Karen was free for lunch almost every day. She usually packed a peanut butter sandwich and ate it at her desk unless someone at the firm, most often Abby, asked her to go out. Lisa Robbins had left for Hong Kong. Karen connected with another law-school classmate, Jennifer Collingswood, who was teaching in a one-year program at Berkeley when Karen first arrived in San Francisco. Jennifer had taken BART into the city, and they'd met for a casual lunch at the Boudin's on Market Street.

But Jennifer left Berkeley to teach at a law school in North Carolina, and Karen hadn't tracked down any other classmates so far.

"I could meet you if we go somewhere not too far from my office," Karen said.

"Pick a place, and I'll meet you there. Any place you like."

Karen thought for a moment, then remembered the restaurants on Belden Place. She chose Café Bastille, the one Lisa Robbins had liked. Brad said he'd make a reservation for 12:30, and Karen agreed to meet him there.

A brilliant sun shone down on Karen as she approached the restaurant. She felt nervous, meeting up with Brad Hertz after so many years. She'd taken a few minutes in the firm's restroom to run a comb through her reddish-brown hair and add some bright lipstick to her mouth.

How would she look to Brad? Older, of course.

She was damned curious to see what he looked like, too.

Chapter 17

Approaching Café Bastille on foot, Karen tried to allay her nerves. She glanced quickly at her watch. She hadn't allowed enough time to get to the restaurant by 12:30, and she was ten minutes late.

She searched the outside tables and saw a good-looking man smiling tentatively in her direction. Her heart skipped a beat. It was Brad Hertz, she was sure of it, and he looked much as he had in law school. Just fifteen years older....

Like me, Karen thought.

She rushed to the table. Brad stood up, and they hugged. She noticed that he was still slim, unlike a lot of the male lawyers Karen knew, who'd begun adding a paunch only a few years into their sedentary careers. His face had a few more lines, and his light brown hair had thinned a bit, but he still smiled the same warm smile she remembered. She wondered why their relationship had never really taken off during their law-school years. The attraction, the sexual tension, was still there.

"Tell me what's going on with you," Brad said after a server took their order. He remembered that she'd started out on Wall Street in New York, but he'd lost track of where she'd gone from there. "Lisa told me you were in Chicago for a few years, but after your husband died, you decided to move out here."

"That's right," Karen said. Karen went on to fill in some of the details of the past fifteen years. She told him how she'd met and fallen in love with Jon, explained why she'd moved to Chicago to be with him, added that she'd decided to focus on estate-planning while working there.

She beamed when she told him about Davi, leaving out any mention of her abduction.

"What about you?" Karen asked. "Didn't you start out in D.C.?"

"Right. I worked at the State Department for a while, then joined a law firm. But I got divorced a couple of years ago and decided to leave the firm. I work now for a think tank that focuses on international relations. The job involves a lot of travel, and I finally got a chance to come to San Francisco."

"I'm glad you did," Karen said, smiling. She tried to keep from grinning. It was exciting to sit across a table from Brad Hertz, exhilarating to reconnect with someone she'd been so attracted to during law school.

They consumed with great relish the *coq au vin* and *salade nicoise* they'd ordered, then lingered a while over *crème brulée* and small cups of strong coffee. Karen glanced at her watch again, remembering that she had to head back to her office. When she looked up, Brad was staring at her with the sort of look on a man's face she hadn't witnessed in a while. Was he interested in pursuing the conversation, in ordering more coffee, so they could linger even longer at their table?

Suddenly, Brad grabbed Karen's hand. "Karen, would you like to take a walk with me? Show me some of the sights near here? I'd love to spend a little more time with you."

Karen's heart started to race. Brad's hand on hers was unexpected, exciting.

"Okay. Why not?" she said, smiling. "I can get back to work a little late."

Brad paid their bill, and they began to stroll down the streets near Belden Place. Brad took her hand in his as Karen led them in the direction of the Ferry Building. Brad suddenly stopped. In the middle of Post Street, he leaned over and kissed her.

Karen was startled, unable to speak. Her heart was racing even faster now.

He kissed me....

"Karen," Brad said, interrupting her thoughts. "I'm staying at a hotel just a few blocks from here. Would you like to see my room? Maybe have a drink with me there...."

Karen hesitated. What was happening? She felt a powerful attraction to Brad. It was almost as though the last fifteen years hadn't happened, and she was falling for him all over again. Falling hard.

Chapter 18

Hand in hand, Karen and Brad walked up Montgomery Street to the Palace Hotel, crossing Market Street not far from Karen's office building. Her heart was pounding as they entered the venerable hotel's lobby and took an elevator to Brad's floor.

Karen felt shaky as they entered his room. What was she doing, following him to his hotel room like this? It seemed insane, impulsive, like so many decisions she'd made when she was younger. Hadn't she learned to make wiser decisions by this point in her life?

Brad's hand still gripping hers, he turned and kissed her again. And again.

He led her to a beige chair near the window and seated himself in its twin across from her. "Karen," he began, "I'm so attracted to you. I think I always was. What happened? Why didn't we connect when we were students?'

"I don't know," Karen replied. "I had an enormous crush on you, and we went out a couple of times, but after a while, we drifted apart. I'd see you around the law school, but you seemed to have lost interest in me."

Brad looked out the window, thinking. Then he turned to her again. "I remember now. I remember what happened." He paused. "I'd met Ellen by then."

"Ellen?"

"My ex. She was a grad student in history. Her roommate was dating a friend of mine, and he introduced us. She and I...."

"You don't have to tell me the details, Brad. What happened happened."

"I just want to explain.... Explain why you and I never....," Brad said. His mouth tightened. "Ellen went after me in a big way. She was smart and pretty, and I started dating her exclusively. By the time you and I graduated, she'd pressured me into getting engaged. We got married a year later."

Karen nodded. She remembered seeing his wedding announcement in *The New York Times*. It had saddened her, but it didn't really surprise her. By then, she hadn't heard from Brad for over a year.

Brad glanced down at his hands, a look of intense regret on his face. He looked up at Karen again and resumed talking. "I was stupid, Karen. I never should have married her. The marriage was okay at first, but after the first few years we grew apart. We stopped liking each other...."

"That sounds awful," Karen said. *So different from my marriage to Jon.*

"But one good thing came out of our marriage. My son Josh. He's 12 now, a great kid. Raising him kept Ellen and me together...until things got really rocky. We finally split up two years ago."

"I'm so sorry, Brad."

"Maybe, maybe, if I'd stuck with you, things would have turned out differently."

"Maybe...."

Brad rose from his chair and approached Karen, grasping her hands in his. "Maybe it's not too late, Karen. Maybe we can pick up where we left off..."

Karen pulled her hands away. She rose from her chair and started walking toward the door, shaking her head. "This is too sudden, Brad. It's been a long time. Too long."

"I know, I know. But...." Brad pulled Karen toward him and began to kiss her again. "Why don't we try spending this afternoon together and see where it goes...."

Karen's heart sped up. She paused, uncertain what to do. It was exciting, thrilling really, to be in a man's arms again....

She suddenly remembered her first romantic encounter with Jon. They'd picnicked at a small lake near Walden. After a quick swim, they'd shared a crazy, impetuous, totally unpredictable plunge into sexual desire. They'd let intimacy progress fast, and it was wonderful.

The next morning, she'd briefly questioned whether that impetuous plunge had been the right thing to do, but it turned out to be exactly right. It led to having Jon in her life for the next eight years. Eight astonishingly happy years.

Maybe it wasn't entirely crazy to fall into Brad's arms the way she'd fallen into Jon's. Maybe....

Brad began fumbling with the buttons on her blouse, steering her gently toward the king-sized bed. Karen made a weak attempt at protesting. "It's been a long time for me, Brad. I haven't gone to bed with anyone since Jon died.... Maybe we should cool things off, wait a while...."

"I won't pressure you to do anything you don't want to do, Karen. But isn't this something you want to do? Don't you want to do this right now?"

Karen's protests evaporated as Brad continued to remove her blouse, then her bra. He was breathing hard, and when he saw her breasts, he moaned with desire. "You have beautiful breasts," he whispered. They fell onto the bed together, undressing each other, exploring each other's bodies. Karen was melting, melting....

She lay back on the bed and opened herself up to Brad, felt him enter her, felt his powerful thrust inside her. It had been a long time since she'd shared her body with a man. Four long years since Jon died, leaving her distraught, uncertain she would ever want to make love with a man again.

During that four-year drought, her thoughts had sometimes drifted back to the heart-pounding thrill of sex with a caring lover like Jon. She'd wondered whether she'd ever find anyone who would raise her to the heights of sexual fulfillment the way Jon had.

"Your mouth, your eyes...," Brad was saying. Hearing him speak this way, she thought it might be possible. Brad aroused in her the same sexual exhilaration Jon had. His hands caressing her breasts, his obvious pleasure as he entered her, then brought her to a climax, his pleasure as he climaxed at the same time...maybe it really was possible.

Finishing, they separated for a moment, then turned and held onto each other again. "Karen," Brad began. He was still breathing fast, still recovering from their love-making. "I've thought about doing that for a long time."

Karen was silent. *What was he saying?*

"You and I...we should have found each other back in law school. We should have been together back then. And never stopped. I should have...."

"Don't look back, Brad. We can't change the past. But maybe, as you said, we can pick up where we left off."

Without any clothes covering her, Karen suddenly felt a chill. She extended her hands to grab the garments Brad had removed, found them, and began dressing.

"Yes, that's exactly what we should do," Brad said. "Pick up where we left off. Beginning today...beginning with what happened today." A smile began to spread across his face. "Beginning now." He grabbed Karen's hand and brought it to his lips, kissing it with a besotted smile on his face. He pulled her whole body toward him and kissed her again, this time on the lips. Karen began melting again, melting....

Suddenly Karen came to her senses. She glanced at her watch. Nearly three o'clock. "Brad, I have to get going. Get back to work."

His smile vanished. "Right," he said. "I understand."

They finished dressing and rose to leave the room. Brad grabbed her arm and looked plaintively at her. "When will we see each other again? I have to get on a plane and go back to D.C. tonight."

Karen paused. "I don't know. I really don't know. Will you be coming back here?"

"I don't have any trips planned right now, but I'll try to come up with some reason to get back here."

Karen nodded, wondering how soon that would be.

"There's always weekends," Brad added. "I could come out here on a Friday night and stay till Sunday. That would give us a whole weekend together."

He looked hopeful, but Karen knew that plan wouldn't work. A brief weekend encounter, now and then. How could that lead anywhere?

She nodded again, trying to look encouraging. "Sure. You could do that." She turned to leave, and Brad followed her out of the room.

In the hotel lobby, they said a brief good-bye, Brad repeating how they'd meet again the next time he was in San Francisco. Karen smiled and nodded one more time. Then she straightened her shoulders and left, walking back to her office with a cascade of questions tumbling through her brain.

Will I really see him again? When? A weekend?

How can we create any kind of relationship, with him on the East Coast and me in San Francisco?

It had been a wonderful afternoon, a beautiful interlude in her otherwise static existence. A static existence altered only by the threats of a psycho abductor.

And now the interlude was over, *fini*. She'd return to her by-now familiar pattern of all day at work, followed by evenings at home with Davi. To trying to track down the psycho who had traumatized Davi and threatened Karen herself.

Without much hope for the kind of love she'd had with Jon. The kind of love she'd thought, for one stunning moment, that she might have had with Brad.

Chapter 19

Karen's brief interlude with Brad reminded her how alone she often felt.

Of course she had Davi's daily companionship, so she didn't see herself as one of "the lonely people" Paul McCartney sang about in "Eleanor Rigby."

But she needed to have more adults in her life, and she'd found it hard to make new friends. The lawyers at Franklin & Cooper were preoccupied with their own lives. They were usually friendly but only when their schedules allowed.

Especially Abby Plummer. Karen and Abby spent occasional lunchtimes together, eating or shopping. But it was clear to Karen that Abby's primary focus was on her work and her own family in the East Bay.

Another woman, Zerlina Hilton, had begun working at the firm. Karen soon learned she was a bright UCLA Law grad who'd just moved from L.A. to practice with Franklin & Cooper. Another possible friend? Karen spent some time visiting her office and chatting with her for a while. Karen admired Zerlina's warm honey-toned skin, so different from Karen's own freckle-prone skin.

Zerlina had grown up in Oakland and still had many friends and family close by, so becoming bosom buddies seemed unlikely. But Karen resolved to make the effort.

One morning they took a break and chatted over coffee at Starbucks. After comparing the relative merits of their offices at the firm, Karen decided to tell Zerlina what had happened to Davi.

When she learned about Davi's abduction, Zerlina hesitated before speaking. Then she revealed to Karen that she'd worked at the L.A. public defender's office before switching to her L.A. law-firm job, the one Karen already knew about.

During her four years as a public defender, Zerlina had often defended violent criminals and was happy to leave that scene. Now, with that experience in mind, Zerlina gave Karen her perspective on Davi's abduction.

She didn't think Karen should continue to worry about it. "This guy, whoever did it, he sounds troubled and probably mentally ill. But not really violent. He didn't harm Davi physically, did he?"

Karen shook her head.

"It's been a few months since the abduction, right? And nothing else has happened?"

Karen nodded.

"Well, I certainly understand why that note—the one that said 'you're next'—upset you. But my sense is he's not likely to follow up on it," Zerlina said.

Zerlina's reassuring words heartened Karen. If she was right, Karen's fears—for Davi, for herself—could be set aside.

Karen also welcomed having a new friend at the firm. But she couldn't expect Zerlina, with her countless friends and family nearby, to spare a lot of time for her. So Karen knew she had to make still more efforts to find new friends.

Someone else had seemed like a possibility. Liz Allen, a middle-aged mom she'd met at Davi's school, was a busy orthopedic surgeon in San Francisco. They'd chatted together briefly, and Karen had hopes of building a friendship with her. But after a couple of phone calls, the connection between them went nowhere.

Karen wasn't surprised. She could easily imagine how much juggling Liz did, between a busy orthopedic practice and an active child like Davi's schoolmate.

One morning, she suddenly remembered Lisa Robbins's suggestion: the Harvard Club. That had seemed like a good way to meet people. She'd have to check out the club's website again, see which of its new events might interest her.

Maybe she'd look into the possibility of a Princeton alumni group as well. Her undergraduate years at Princeton seemed long ago, and she'd never kept up with any of her college classmates. She'd been too busy with her demanding work as a lawyer and her domestic life as a wife and mother. But maybe it wasn't too late to reconnect with fellow Princeton alums. She'd look into that, too.

In the meantime, wasn't there someone she'd already met at a Harvard event? The guy she'd talked to when she went to the opera with the Harvard Club?

Before Davi was abducted, and Karen's life had changed dramatically as a result.

Karen searched her memory, trying to recall that evening and the two men she'd met just before the opera began. One of them had flirted with her, hadn't he? He'd even hinted that he might want to become her client.

Why haven't I heard from him? Is he waiting to hear from me? Maybe I should take the initiative and track him down.

Karen tried to remember his name. His first name wasn't a run-of-the-mill man's name, like Jack or John. No, it was a little less common, and it began with a "K" sound.

But it didn't start with K. She seemed to remember it started with C.

Was it Carson? Conor? Colin? No, none of those.

It had reminded her of a device.

She searched her memory again. Was it a camera? Was his name...Cameron?

Yes! That was it! Cameron! His friends called him Cam.

His last name...it had reminded her of a famous author. Who?

Karen played more memory games as she brainstormed, trying to come up with authors' names. Dickens? Fitzgerald? Surely not Hemingway. Someone who was still alive....

Karen turned back to the files stacked on her desk. Maybe if I don't try too hard to remember, it will pop up in my brain somehow. I won't focus on it for a while....

Wait. Karen remembered that the author's name had some connection to the law, to lawyers.

Who had written a memorable book about lawyers? Turow? Grisham? Those didn't seem to fit.

Suddenly an image emerged from the recesses of her brain. The image of Gregory Peck in a loose-fitting three-piece suit. Gregory Peck as Atticus Finch in *To Kill a Mockingbird*. The film based on the book by Harper Lee.

Harper...Harper? Yes! Cam's last name was Harper. It was the author's first name, not her last, but that was it. Karen was sure of it.

She glanced at her computer screen and typed her inquiry into White Pages, hoping to find a listing for a Cameron Harper in San Francisco. White Pages produced two names: Cameron Meredith Harper and Cameron A. Harper. Which one had she met?

Cameron Meredith Harper's address was on Jackson Street, and the house number wasn't far from Karen's apartment. Cameron A. Harper was listed somewhere in the Mission.

Karen decided to jot down the first phone number and call that Cam Harper sometime. Ask him whether he was the guy she'd met at the opera, whether he was still interested in becoming her client. She stuck his phone number in her desk drawer, resolving to call him that afternoon, or maybe the next morning.

Cameron Meredith Harper. The name embedded itself in her brain.

By the next morning, Karen couldn't wait to try her luck. She pulled the note with his phone number out of her desk drawer and dialed, prepared to leave a message.

Cam Harper answered the phone right away, and Karen rushed to explain who she was.

"Cam, this is Karen Clark. We met at the opera a few months ago."

Silence. "'The Marriage of Figaro,'" she added. "The Harvard Club event..."

"Oh, yes, Karen. I remember you now."

There was an awkward pause, and Karen jumped in to fill it.

"I was just wondering, Cam. Are you ever downtown at lunchtime? Would you like to meet for lunch sometime?" Her voice was shaky, nervous.

She decided to defer for the moment asking him about planning his estate. That could wait.

Cam responded immediately. "I'd love to meet you for lunch, Karen. Pick a good time, and I'll pick the place."

Karen was delighted by Cam's response. *So he remembers me...and he's eager to see me again.* She was surprised and pleased at the same time.

"How's Friday? At noon?"

"Perfect. Can you meet me at the Tadich Grill? They have wonderful seafood."

Karen wasn't sure where the Tadich Grill was, but she'd look it up. It had to be downtown somewhere.

"Sure. That sounds great."

"See you then, Karen." Cam hung up.

Karen sat back in her office chair, trying to process what had just happened. She'd impulsively called a man she hardly knew, whom she'd briefly spoken to months before, and he'd immediately jumped at the idea of seeing her again.

Suddenly there was someone new in her life. The result of another one of her impulsive decisions.

And who knows? Karen thought. Maybe this time it will turn out to be a good one.

Chapter 20

Another crowded bus ride home, and Karen entered her apartment building, headed once again for the mailboxes. She immediately saw Gordon Whitlock, this time crumpled like a pile of clothes in front of the elevator.

"Gordon!" she said as she approached him. "What happened?"

The elderly man could hardly speak. Karen reached out to him, hoping to help him stand up. He allowed her to grasp his bony hand.

"I stumbled," he said. "Not sure I can get up." Karen put down her handbag and briefcase and used both arms to support him as he attempted to stand. Clutching him, she could feel how frail he was, his jacket hanging off his body as he stood up.

"Gordon, do you want me to call 911?"

"Oh, no! I'm all right now," he assured her.

His eyes narrowed as he scrutinized her face. "You're Karen, aren't you?"

"Yes, that's right," Karen said, nodding her head. "Let me take you to your apartment," she insisted. Still holding onto him with her right hand, she gathered up her things with her other hand, and both of them entered the elevator.

"Which floor, Gordon?" she asked.

"Five. I'm on five."

Karen pressed the button for the fifth floor and emerged from the elevator with Gordon. They walked to his door together, and he fumbled with his keys for a moment until he found the right one.

Karen continued to support him, wanting to help him get settled comfortably in his apartment. They entered his living room, which faced south, like Karen's, allowing brilliant sunshine to brighten the room nearly every day.

Karen led Gordon to a shabby dark tan sofa in the middle of the room, and he collapsed into it. "Are you feeling okay?" she asked. "I don't want to leave you alone unless you feel okay."

Gordon looked up at Karen and smiled a weak smile. "I'm just fine now, dear. But if you could bring me a glass of water, I'd appreciate it."

"Of course!" Karen rushed into his kitchen, found a smudged glass in a cupboard, and filled it with water at the sink.

Walking back into the living room, she noticed photos of small children everywhere, countless frames sitting on top of every available surface in the room. "Who are all these children?" she asked.

"Those are very special children," he said. "I love children, you know."

"Are they your grandchildren, Gordon? Other kids in your family?"

"No, no, just some special children, Karen. My special little friends."

His response struck Karen as odd, especially in light of what Greg Chan had said about an unnamed tenant in her building, but she was eager to leave Gordon and get to her own apartment. "If you're okay, Gordon, I'll leave now. Do you want me to check on you later?"

"No, dear. I'll be fine."

Karen said goodbye and left. On her way to her own apartment on the third floor, she suddenly remembered Gordon's sofa. It was dark tan. Would Davi have described it as brown?

And all those photos of little kids. Who were they? Was Gordon the neighbor Greg Chan had mentioned? He didn't have the strength to grab Davi, did he?

These questions troubled Karen as she turned her key in her lock. But she forgot all about them when she saw Davi again, safe and happy. With sitter Juanita on her way out the door, Karen and Davi cooked a huge quantity of spaghetti with marinara sauce for dinner, planning to fill their hungry stomachs as fast as possible.

*   *.   *

Two days later, Karen ran into Ramsey Boyd in a hallway at the firm. He looked startled to see her. Karen remembered that she'd never followed up with him about going out for coffee. *He probably thinks I've been avoiding him.* Truthfully, she had.

"Karen, how've you been?" he asked, affecting an unconcerned look.

"Pretty good, Ram," she answered, wondering whether she should say something more.

Ram solved her problem. "How about that coffee, Karen?" His tone was cool, not as eager as the last time. *I'll bet he's afraid I'm going to shoot him down again.*

"Sure, Ram," she said, attempting a smile. Karen glanced at her watch, then looked back at Ram. "I could leave for a few minutes right now. What about you?"

"Let's go," he said immediately. He turned and headed for the elevator, Karen rushing to keep up with him.

Once they arrived at Starbucks and located an empty table, they faced each other, waiting for their steaming cups of coffee to cool off. Ram began talking right away.

His conversation immediately struck Karen as odd. Grinning goofily, he started by asking about Davi. "How she's doing?" he said.

Why is he concerned about Davi? Just trying to be nice? But it's a strange way to start finding out about me.

"Okay," Karen answered, then tried to shift the focus to Ram. "What's up with you?"

Ram's face turned grim. He began by saying that he'd just broken up with "a girl named Cindy." A "girl" he'd gone with for a while. "She had a cute little kid, about the same age as your daughter. I loved taking Olivia out for burgers and fries on Saturdays when Cindy was at work. Olivia's cute little friend Carla sometimes came along, too."

As Ram continued, telling her how much he missed seeing these two little girls, Karen felt increasingly uncomfortable.

His fondness for little girls might be perfectly fine, but....

When he started asking about Davi again, Karen knew it was time to end their coffee break. *I can't bear listening to him any longer.*

Karen glanced at her watch and announced she had to get back to work.

Ram didn't protest. They left Starbucks together and returned to the office.

After work, another crowded bus ride later, Karen approached the front door of her apartment building. As she began inserting her key into the door lock, she sensed someone behind her. She slowly turned to see who it was.

What the...? It was Ram. He'd apparently followed her home.

Or else he'd tracked down her home address and found her that way. Either way, his behavior was unsettling.

Karen's heart began pounding. *What's he doing here?*

She knew she had to confront him. "Why are you here?" she demanded.

"I'd like to meet Davi," Ram said. "I thought the three of us could go out for dinner. Wouldn't that be fun?"

Karen tried to catch her breath. *I have to get rid of him. Right now.*

"No, Ram, it wouldn't," she said quickly. "I need this time to chill out after a long day at work. You...you can meet Davi some other time. Not right now."

Her stern response seemed to take Ram by surprise. "I thought we were friends, Karen. I thought it would be...."

"No. Not now, Ram. We'll...we'll pick another time to get together. Maybe on a weekend," she added, trying to keep an even tone. She was worried, not sure what Ram would do if she didn't come up with an acceptable alternative.

"Some other time, Ram. Okay?"

A dejected look had crept across Ram's face, but he seemed somewhat appeased by Karen's suggestion. "Okay, Karen. Another time."

He turned and walked away, leaving Karen standing at the door, trying to calm down before entering the building.

He scares me, she thought. *He may be basically okay, but he frightens me. I don't want him to get anywhere near Davi.*

She turned and finished inserting her key into the lock, entered the lobby, and headed upstairs. She couldn't wait to get inside her apartment and give Davi a great big hug.

Chapter 21

A quick look at the internet turned up what Karen needed to know about the Tadich Grill. It was one of San Francisco's landmark restaurants, dating from 1849 and claiming to be the oldest continuously run restaurant in the city. It had taken the name of its founder, John Tadich, in 1887 and had thrived ever since. Zagat's review noted its famous grilled seafood, and Karen could hardly wait to sample some.

A line had formed on California Street by the time Karen arrived at noon on Friday, and she searched for a familiar face. Toward the back of the line, she saw Derek Cooper, one of the partners at Franklin & Cooper, accompanied by Ramsey Boyd.

Derek and Ram glimpsed her and began whispering to each other. Karen's stomach felt queasy, remembering her recent encounters with Ram, but she waved half-heartedly and continued to look for Cam Harper.

When she didn't see him anywhere in line, she tried walking through the entrance and found him already inside, standing by the host's desk. "I got here early, Karen. This place fills up fast," he explained. "I have a nice table waiting for us."

His large frame dwarfed hers. Karen had almost forgotten how tall and well-built he was. He grabbed her elbow and escorted her to a table in a far corner, a quieter location than most in the noisy jam-packed restaurant.

"Order anything you like," he said, grinning. "The tab's on me."

Karen perused the menu, chose grilled halibut, and sat back in her chair, appraising Cam. He was just as she remembered from their brief meeting at the opera. Piercing blue eyes beneath neatly groomed eyebrows and a salt-and-pepper beard still dominated his appearance.

Karen liked his looks, but was he a bit too eager, the way he'd grabbed her elbow? She knew she should be delighted to have a man like him interested in her. She wanted to get to know him better.

Cam seemed to have the same idea. "Tell me about yourself, Karen," he said. "You went to Harvard, right?"

"Right. I went to the law school. What about you?"

"I went to the college. But quite a few years before you, I suspect!" He laughed heartily. "I finished in '77."

Karen nodded. That made him about ten years older than she was. She wondered whether he'd ever been married, was still married, had any kids. She was about to ask when he began probing her first.

"Did you tell me you're a recent transplant to San Francisco?" he asked. Karen didn't remember whether she'd actually told him that. Maybe she had. "Where did you move from?"

"Chicago. I worked at a law firm there...."

"Chicago!" Cam exclaimed. "I grew up in Chicago!"

Karen felt some sort of acknowledgment was required. She smiled, nodding.

"I don't need to ask why you moved, Karen," Cam said. "Those winters.... I don't miss those brutal winters at all."

The grilled seafood arrived, and as Karen ate her perfectly prepared halibut, she glanced around the restaurant, admiring the beautiful wood paneling surrounding their table. She ate quickly, unsure that she wanted to spend a long lunch with Cam. Their chitchat—mostly about restaurants in San Francisco—didn't interest her very much. Karen wanted to change the subject, but he was one of those men who liked to hear themselves talk and dominated a conversation with their own pronouncements. So her attempt to talk about the opera's latest offerings didn't get very far.

Even worse, she didn't think there was any real spark between them. Too bad, she thought. I was hoping he'd be a wonderful new friend, maybe even a romantic interest. But in light of the rather dull conversation so far, that didn't seem likely.

Karen wondered whether he remembered mentioning that he might like to be her client. She was about to ask about that when he shifted to something else entirely.

"You seem unhappy, Karen," he said abruptly.

He must have detected how bored she was. But this crude attempt to connect with her struck her as highly inept.

"Unhappy? Not really." She smiled, trying to stay friendly, at least for now.

"Are you happy at your job? What about at home?"

Karen was startled by these questions, coming out of the blue. But maybe they weren't entirely unpredictable. The two of them were supposed to be learning about each other, weren't they? He had simply plunged into asking how her new life in San Francisco was going. Just doing it rather awkwardly.

"I'm really happy at my job," she said quickly, hoping he'd stay with that subject and not pry into her home life. She was hoping to segue to the possibility that he might become her client. "Everyone at the firm has been very warm and friendly, and I like the work. As you know, I focus on estate-planning. You even mentioned...."

"But something's troubling you, Karen. I can tell," Cam interrupted. His piercing blue eyes narrowed as he scrutinized her face. "Is it your family? Your husband, a child you're worried about?"

Even more startled than before, Karen hardly knew what to say. "I...my husband...my husband died a few years ago," she said, her voice shaking. Losing Jon was still painful, and she didn't like to talk about it.

"Oh, I'm so sorry to hear that, Karen." Cam's face suddenly looked empathetic. "I've lost someone close to me, too. My mother died several years ago, and I still think about her every day. A loss like that...you never really get over it."

Karen nodded in agreement.

"Is that what troubles you?" Cam continued. "I understand so well how you feel. But I hope you know it's not healthy to keep dwelling on the past. At a certain point, we do what we need to, to deal with our grief. Then we just have to move on."

Karen nodded again. She'd heard that kind of hackneyed advice a million times. She *had* moved on, she'd moved—literally--to San Francisco, and she was doing what she could to make a new life for herself. "You're absolutely right, Cam. That's exactly what I'm trying to do. That's why..."

"But you still have some anguish in your life, don't you, Karen? Something that's disturbing you. You can confide in me. Maybe it would help to talk about it." Cam looked intensely into her eyes. He seemed to be probing, searching for what was troubling her.

Karen hesitated. Should she tell Cam about Davi? He seemed so sympathetic, so eager to help. Maybe if she confided in him, maybe it would help somehow.

"Well, Cam, there is something else," she said tentatively. "I don't know if I should tell you because...because the police are still investigating, but...."

Cam's eyes opened wide. He stared at Karen, taking her hand in his. "Karen, you can tell me. You can tell me anything. Your secrets are safe with me."

Cam's hand felt a bit clammy, and she wished she could remove her own from his grasp. But he seemed sincerely interested in helping her, so she plunged ahead. "My daughter...Davi...she's eight years old. She was abducted by someone on Market Street in August."

"Abducted! How terrible!" Cam's face registered shock, concern. "Was she harmed?"

"No," Karen said, "thankfully, she wasn't harmed physically. But she was traumatized by what happened."

"Is she back home with you?"

"We found her the next morning, and she's been home with me ever since. She's back in school now, and she seems to be doing well. Almost back to normal."

"Thank God," he said. "Do you know who did it?" Another look of concern covered Cam's face.

"No, no, the police are still investigating. But what kind of person would do such a thing? Who would want to terrify a child like that?" Karen's eyes filled with tears, and she stifled the urge to cry. She hardly knew this man. Why was she telling him what had happened to her daughter?

Cam squeezed her hand. "She's home with you, Karen. That's all that matters, isn't it? She's home now, and doing well." He smiled empathetically again.

It occurred to Karen that everything she'd said hadn't led to his mentioning a wife or children of his own. Only his mother. *I guess he's never married.*

But instead of asking him about it, Karen decided to change the conversation. *I'll ask him now about becoming my client. Why not? He's the one who suggested it in the first place.*

"Cam," she began, "I can't help wondering about something you said when we met at the opera. You said you might like me to look over your will. Remember?"

Cam looked away, focusing on a nearby table filled with noisy patrons.

Was he serious when he said that? Or was it simply a carrot to dangle in front of me?

Cam turned back to face Karen. "Yes, that's right! I'd almost forgotten. My will probably could use looking over," he smiled. "Give me a day or two to track it down. I'll give you a call, and we can set up a time to review it together. How does that sound?"

Karen's discomfort with Cam dissipated, and she nodded eagerly. *Bringing in a new client would boost my standing at the firm.* "That sounds great, Cam. You have my number?"

"Sure do." He squeezed her hand again. His clammy hand still felt unpleasant, but the prospect of a new client overwhelmed any hesitation she might have otherwise felt.

Karen could barely swallow the gooey dessert Cam ordered, then insisted that they share. When the plate was empty, they both rose from the table and left the Tadich Grill together, Cam promising to call Karen as soon as he could track down his current will.

*　　*　　*

The following Monday, Karen got a call from Cam.

Is he ready to review his will with me? Her luck with him seemed to be panning out.

"Karen, I finally found a copy of my will. Why don't you come to my house, and we can look at it together."

Come to your house?

"Can't you bring it to my office? That's where we normally meet our clients. I can arrange my schedule to meet you here tomorrow."

"No, no, I can't come downtown this week. I'm expecting some important calls from Asia, and I don't want to leave the house. I can explain when I see you."

Karen hesitated. It seemed highly unusual to meet with a new client at his house. Or was it? She wasn't sure. She could check with Abby....

"Come to my house, Karen, and we can talk here," Cam insisted. "I'm at 2515 Jackson Street. Do you know where that is?"

"Is that near Alta Plaza Park?"

"That's right. I'm on Jackson just west of the corner with Steiner. Why don't you come right over?"

Karen hesitated again. "Cam...I...I don't think I...."

"Why not, Karen? We can talk here without any interruptions. It'll be much better than trying to talk at your office."

Karen was still reluctant to meet with Cam at his house, but maybe it would be all right. *Bringing in a new client would be a feather in my cap. And he seems legit. He's Harvard and all that.*

She decided to tell Cam she'd meet with him at his house. It appeared to be the only way to get him on board as a new client. *I'll check with Abby before I leave. If she doesn't think it's a good idea, I can always call him and cancel.*

"I can't leave work right now, Cam," she said. "Give me a couple of hours. I'll come by this afternoon. I can walk there."

"Great. I'll see you then."

Karen rushed to Abby's office and hastily explained why she wanted to take off for a few hours. "I'm hoping to add him as a client," she said, her voice still uncertain. "What do you think?"

"That sounds great, Karen. Go ahead and meet with this guy. It's all right to meet him at his house. I've done that once or twice myself," Abby said.

"And don't worry," she added reassuringly. "Everything here will be perfectly fine here without you."

So meeting with Cam at his house would be all right after all. And Karen knew she didn't need to worry about Davi's well-being. Juanita would be picking her up after school, as planned, and staying with her till Karen's usual getting-home time.

Karen hurried out of the office and hailed a taxi to speed her home as fast as possible. Once there, she laced on her Reeboks and set out for 2515 Jackson Street.

Hoping that Cam Harper would prove to be a valuable new client.

Chapter 22

As she walked down Jackson Street, passing Steiner, Karen glanced at Alta Plaza Park. The lush green park always reminded her of a film set in San Francisco in the '70s, the screwball comedy "What's Up, Doc?" She'd heard that Barbra Streisand & company had chipped some of the park's concrete steps during the filming of a hilarious chase scene, and she always wondered which of the steps had been damaged back then.

Now her memory of the film and Streisand's crazy antics in it was a helpful distraction. Despite Abby Plummer's assurances, Karen had to admit she felt somewhat apprehensive about meeting with Cam Harper at his house.

Cam had been cordial to her, had even flirted with her during their two encounters. And now he offered her the possibility of becoming her client. But she still felt uncertain she was doing the right thing by venturing to see him outside of her office. Once again she was being impulsive, hoping this attempt to wrangle a new client would be successful.

Karen reached the stunning Victorian mansion at 2515 Jackson Street and climbed seventeen green wooden steps to a shiny green door facing Jackson. She rang the doorbell and waited. Nothing. She rang it again.

Finally she heard someone approach the door from inside. Was it Cam? Maybe someone else would welcome her instead.

Cam opened the door himself. "Karen!" he exclaimed. "I'm delighted you could make it." His face beamed as he perused Karen from head to toe. Karen felt uneasy in light of his scrutiny, the kind lecherous males frequently directed at her.

"Come in, come in!" Cam said. "I'm sorry Dora isn't here today— it's her day off—or she would be fussing over you, bringing you tea, that sort of thing." So there would be no household employee, no one in the house except Karen and Cam. "But I can make you some tea if you like. Come into the kitchen with me...," Cam added.

"Oh, no, please don't bother," Karen hastened to assure him. "I'm fine. I'd like to begin reviewing your will...." She didn't want to prolong this session any longer than necessary. And the image of standing near Cam while he prepared tea in his kitchen was distinctly unappealing.

"Then let's go into my study. We can sit there and chat for a while," he said, smiling. He ushered Karen through a living room filled with heavy Victorian furniture and into a cheerful study overlooking the bay.

The beige walls were covered with an array of framed artwork, some of which looked like originals and were probably valuable. Cam appeared to have acquired so much artwork that some pieces hadn't even made it onto the walls and still sat on the floor, awaiting a space whenever he got tired of what was already displayed.

The view through the wraparound windows was spectacular, and Karen wondered how Cam got anything done with the distraction of the Bay view just outside his windows. The Golden Gate Bridge gleamed bright orange in the sun. "Wow," Karen said, almost without thinking. "You have a fabulous view. The bridge...."

"Yes, I really love my view," Cam admitted. "This room was a drab, rather ordinary space when I bought the house. I called in a great local architect and a really sharp interior designer, and together they transformed this room. I spend most of my time here. The living room is an over-decorated disaster, pretty much as I found it when I bought the house. But I'm in there so seldom I've never bothered to change it."

Karen nodded, trying to think how to change the subject and get back to the real reason she'd made this trip.

Cam solved the problem for her. "You wanted to discuss my will, right?"

"Yes, yes, that's right. That's why I'm here. I'd like to review your will and give you some feedback on it."

"Of course, of course," he said. He seated himself behind his desk, a mid-twentieth-century teak that was probably worth a small fortune fifty years later. "Please sit down."

He gestured, indicating that Karen should take a seat on the overstuffed velvet sofa that faced his desk. Karen sank into the sofa and waited for Cam to begin. Her eye fell on a lonely framed photo on a small shelf behind his desk. The subject was a 30ish woman, dressed in a '50s-style mid-calf-length dress with a narrow waist—looking like a female star in a Hitchcock film from that era. *Was that a child she was holding? Was it Cam?*

Karen looked back at Cam. He was staring at her.

Maybe he'll finally say something about his will.

"After I found my will," Cam said, "I contacted my lawyer. The one who drew it up a couple of years ago. He assured me that it's still in good shape, and I don't need to change it in any way."

What...? Wasn't the promise of changing his will the reason she was here?

"I'm sorry," Cam was saying, "but he told me he expected me to remain as his client after all."

Karen's heart sank at the news. *Why did suggest he might want me to revise his will? Was he hoping to get closer to me this way?*

He seemed interested in me at the opera. But did he sense my lack of interest in him when we met for lunch? Is that why he decided to make this awkward attempt to connect with me?

She looked around the room, trying to think of a polite way to get out of his clutches. His reason for luring her to his house amounted to exactly nothing, and she felt increasingly uneasy.

He'd started humming "My Kind of Town, Chicago Is" as she glanced at some of the artwork on the walls and along the carpeted floor. Maybe she could mention that she liked one of the pieces. She could get up to view it more closely, then beat a hasty retreat.

Karen tried to extract herself from the overstuffed sofa so she could approach the framed artwork. Pushing against the sofa's velvet cushions, she suddenly noticed its color.

Brown. Karen's heart skipped a beat.

A brown sofa...that was something Davi remembered. A brown sofa.

Maybe she was being irrational, but Karen suddenly felt nervous. She wanted to leave the room, to get away from Cam as fast as possible.

Why do I feel so nervous? I'm sitting on a brown sofa. That's why.

But could this really be the room where Davi slept on a brown sofa? Where she was forced to stay for so many hours?

No, it can't be...it can't be....

Cam was staring at her with an odd look on his face. "What's the matter, Karen? You look like you've seen a ghost. Has something frightened you?"

Karen's need to know trumped her fear. "I *am* frightened, Cam."

"What's frightened you? I don't understand." Cam stared blankly at Karen, as though he had no idea what she was talking about.

"Something about this room frightens me."

"This room? What do you mean, Karen?" The expressionless look remained on Cam's face.

Karen paused before she spoke. She wanted to choose her words carefully. "I think my daughter may have been forced to stay in this room." she said. "Because of you, or because of someone else. Someone you're protecting."

Maybe he's protecting that friend of his. The one who was with Cam at the opera. Ken, wasn't it? Ken Pryce? Pryce with a "y"?

Cam sat back in his chair. Now he began to smile. A weird sort of smile.

"I'm impressed, Karen. How did you figure that out?"

Karen paused again, her heart pounding. *So I'm right.... Something did happen here....*

She quickly blurted out how Davi remembered sleeping on a brown sofa. How Karen suspected that Cam had never intended to discuss his will with her at all. How it suddenly seemed possible that he knew something about Davi's abduction. And he had lured Karen to his house because he did.

"Why *did* you lure me here with your talk about your will? Why?" Cam was silent.

"If you know anything about Davi's abduction, I beg you, Cam, please tell me."

He stared at Karen for a long time, the same weird smile on his face. "All right, Karen," he finally said. "I will. In fact, I'm happy to explain."

Happy? Karen could barely believe she'd heard Cam correctly. *He's happy to explain...?*

"Happy?" she repeated.

"Yes. Happy. Because now I can tell someone the whole story. The reasons behind everything I've done for the past six years."

"Six years?" *What was he saying?*

"I'll start at the beginning, Karen...."

His voice began to drift off as he turned to gaze at the view outside his windows. He sighed deeply, then turned to Karen and began speaking again.

Chapter 23

"You remember, Karen…," Cam began. "I told you I'm from Chicago."

Karen nodded warily.

He opened a drawer in his desk and pulled out a meerschaum pipe, a tin of pipe tobacco, and a box of matches. He filled the pipe and lighted it before beginning to speak again. "I was raised in what people call a broken home. It was broken all right. My father walked out on my mother, married his secretary, and moved to Scottsdale. He never showed any interest in me after that, and Mother essentially became a single mother. Fortunately, my father was willing to give her a lot of money, so we were quite comfortable when I was growing up."

What was all this about?

"Mother didn't want me to attend a public school, so she sent me to the Latin School, where most of my classmates were snobby ultra-rich types who by and large wanted nothing to do with me. Maybe it was my appearance or my…, shall we say, my demeanor that put them off. I never knew why. But I retreated into my books and my music… I play the violin, Karen. Did you know that?"

Karen shook her head. *Violin? What did that have to do with anything?*

"I was happy, as happy as I suppose any unpopular kid is. Mother took good care of me, showering me with attention, taking me to the opera, the theater, concerts, movies. I was her constant companion, and she was mine.

116

"When it was time for me to go off to college, she wanted me to stay in Chicago, but I rejected that idea. Here was a chance for me to leave Chicago and start a new life somewhere else, somewhere I might find a few classmates who didn't hate me on sight. You can understand why I wanted to leave, can't you?"

Karen nodded. "Of course," she said. "You wanted to make a fresh start...." *The way I wanted to make a fresh start in San Francisco.*

"Right. I was a bright kid, Karen, and I wanted to study science. All kinds of new technology were just getting off the ground. I began to hear about the brand-new field of computer science. It sounded like a good field for someone like me, someone who didn't relate well to the popular kids. I thought I'd meet other kids like me and finally make a bunch of friends. So when I was accepted at Harvard, I jumped at the chance to leave home and begin my new life there."

Karen kept nodding, encouraging him to continue.

"Mother didn't like it, but she accepted my choice and paid every cent of my expensive education. I did well at Harvard, of course, mastering the subject matter, making a few friends. Did you know Bill Gates was at Harvard about the same time I was? Unfortunately, I never met him. He dropped out after two years. But leaving Harvard didn't stand in the way of his success, did it?"

Karen nodded again. *Bill Gates? Where was this going?*

"Thanks to how well I did at Harvard, I gradually came to think I could become a self-made millionaire myself someday and not dependent on Mother anymore. I still loved her, of course. I loved her deeply. But

I also loved my life at Harvard and looked forward to the opportunities that might follow. I stuck around Cambridge for a while, switching to MIT to get my Ph.D.

"After that, I headed for Silicon Valley. It had already taken off as the place for a computer nerd like me to hang out. And sure enough, after working for some other guys for a few years, I launched my own startup. It made a fortune. I later sold it for twenty-six million dollars."

Cam stared at Karen, watching to see her reaction. She obliged him by widening her eyes and nodding some more. He seemed satisfied and resumed talking.

"I liked my life in Palo Alto. I liked it a lot. I got into venture capitalism down there, funding some other guys' startups—I still do--and I've done really well financially. But after a while, I decided to move to San Francisco. To enjoy city life again.

"I had no desire to return to Chicago, but San Francisco offered all the things I'd relished in Chicago and frankly missed. I got a great deal on this house—bought it when the market was down—and I've never been sorry I became a San Franciscan. Better late than never, I always say."

Cam grinned at Karen, hoping for a response.

Why is he telling me all this? What does any of this have to do with Davi? Or me?

Her heart was pounding, but she wanted him to keep talking, so she obliged him once again by smiling and nodding.

"Mother missed me, of course. For years, she pleaded with me to come back to Chicago. I'd visit her a few times a year, but my life was here, in San Francisco. She didn't want to uproot herself and move here, but without me in Chicago, her life was pretty empty. When she finally realized I was never coming back, she made some changes. She moved to a smaller apartment, a condo on Lake Shore Drive, near Belmont Harbor. Know where that is?"

Karen nodded again. She'd never become completely familiar with Chicago, but she did recall the area around Belmont Harbor. It wasn't far from Lincoln Park, near the first apartment she'd shared with Jon, where they'd later taken Davi to the zoo.

"She also decided to make a life for herself. She joined a book club, and she began volunteering at a local hospital. St. Elsa's. Have you heard of it?"

This time Karen shook her head. The only hospital she knew was the one in Evanston where Jon was affiliated. Where Davi was born. Where Jon had died.

"St. Elsa's was within walking distance of Mother's apartment, and pretty soon she was walking there once a week to work as a volunteer. The place is run by a bunch of Catholic nuns, and even though Mother wasn't Catholic, she got along very well with the nuns who ran the volunteer program. They asked her to call a list of names they drew up. A list of disabled people. Mother would call to check up on them on Thursday mornings. She liked making those calls, and she'd tell me about it whenever I phoned her. She loved the idea that she was helping others…something she'd never really done before."

Karen nodded again, but her discomfort level was rising.

How did a hospital run by a bunch of nuns figure into Davi's abduction? I thought this story would lead somewhere, but it hasn't. I should get out of here. As soon as I can.

Karen glanced around the room again, trying to come up with a plausible way to escape.

Cam seemed totally oblivious of Karen's discomfort. His pipe had gone out, so he took a moment to relight it. Then he blithely went on with his story. "So every Thursday morning Mother walked to the hospital, put her things away in a locker in the volunteer room, and got ready to make her phone calls. Only one morning…."

Cam's face suddenly changed, and his breathing speeded up. He appeared to be furious about whatever had happened.

"One morning, she was in the volunteer room, combing her hair in front of a mirror, when another volunteer came charging into the room to use the phone. A lot of people didn't have a cell phone yet, and he must have known about the phone on the table at the far end of the room. He…he was…." Cam totally lost his composure and could barely speak.

Karen waited. She had to admit that she wanted to hear what happened next.

Cam pulled himself together and went on. "This man, this man, was twice my mother's size. She weighed barely a hundred pounds, and we later learned that this miserable human being, this Morris Andretti, weighed two-twenty. More than twice her size."

Cam paused.

"What happened next, Cam?"

"He...he knocked her down! He was in such a goddamned hurry to get to the phone, he knocked her down. This tiny older woman, half his size, he pushed her out of his way, and she fell. She fell."

Karen was beginning to understand Cam's rage.

"When I finally got to see her, she told me he hit her with such force--that's the phrase she used--he hit her with such force, he knocked her down. All she was doing was standing there, in front of the mirror, combing her hair...." Cam choked up, unable to go on.

"Was she hurt?"

He sat there for a moment, silent, then pulled himself together. "Was she hurt? Yeah, she was hurt all right. She broke her hip, Karen. Her hip. You know what that means, don't you?"

Karen nodded. She'd read somewhere that a broken hip can lead to all sorts of unfortunate results.

"It was the beginning of the end for her, Karen. The beginning of the end...."

"When did you get to see her?"

"I flew to Chicago as soon as I could. Took the redeye. Rushed to her bedside from O'Hare. They were making a big fuss over her, those nuns, acting like they cared. Some doctor came in, told me the x-rays had shown she needed hip surgery right away. So they'd gone ahead and done it before I got there. He said she'd be fine.

"But Karen, she...she wasn't fine."

"Did something go wrong during the surgery?"

"No, no, the surgery went okay. But two days later, while she lay in that fucking hospital bed, she had a heart attack."

"What? A heart attack?"

Cam nodded. "The doctor said it was caused by the stress of the surgery. Happens in something like twenty percent of the patients who have hip surgery at her age."

"What bad luck for your mother! Having a heart attack on top of the broken hip," Karen said.

She felt sympathy for Cam, and for his mother. What an unjust reward for doing a good deed. For working as a volunteer in that hospital, only to be knocked down and injured by an oaf who recklessly barged into the office, interested only in making his phone call.

"Bad luck? Hardly!" Cam said, raising his voice. "Andretti— Andretti and the others were responsible for what happened to her!"

Cam's sudden agitation frightened Karen. *I need to change his focus somehow.* "Did she recover from the heart attack? At least she was in the hospital when it happened." *Unlike my darling Jon.* "Weren't they able to help her?"

Tears had welled up in Cam's eyes and began to slither down his cheeks. "Oh, yeah, they helped her," he said sarcastically. "Between that quack doctor and those bitches who called themselves nuns, they fussed over her and pretended to help. But her life was never the same. She left the hospital with a weakened heart and a walker. She never really recovered."

"That's terrible...." Cam's story had transformed him from frightening to sympathetic.

I can relate to his experience. But still...where is he going with this?

"She was in and out of the hospital after that. Congestive heart failure, they called it. She'd never been sick before. Never. And I...I felt guilty, Karen."

"Why? You had nothing to do with her being injured, having the heart attack...."

"But I wasn't there to help her, Karen. Maybe I could have done something to make sure she got the best surgeon, the best doctors. Maybe she didn't have to have the heart attack...if she'd been in a better hospital with better nurses. I could afford to give her the best. But I wasn't there, Karen. By the time I got to Chicago, she'd already had the surgery, and she had to stay in that fucking hospital.

"I felt so guilty, Karen."

He felt guilty. Of course he did.

"If only I hadn't moved to California, if only I'd stayed in Chicago, maybe this never would have happened...."

As she watched Cam and listened to his story, a powerful sadness enveloped Karen.

I know all about guilt.

She could try to make Cam feel better, try to assure him there was nothing he could have done to change what happened.

But she couldn't. Her own feelings of guilt still haunted her.

"If only...if only...."

She knew those words all too well.

Chapter 24

For a moment, Karen and Cam sat in his beautiful office overlooking San Francisco Bay, both unable to speak.

I have to process this, Karen thought. *This sad, sad story about his mother...how does it relate to Davi?*

Shaky and nervous, Karen summoned up her courage and addressed him.

"Cam, "she began, "what happened to your mother was terrible. I can understand why it upset you so much. But please tell me—tell me what it has to do with Davi."

He continued to sit there, looking grim.

He's focused on what happened to his mother and how guilty he feels as a result. But what about Davi?

Once again Karen contemplated trying to leave. But she wanted some answers before she took off.

"Cam, please go on. What happened to your mother after she left the hospital?"

He glanced down at his desk and picked up his meerschaum pipe. It needed relighting, but he just looked at it, then put it back on the desk. He finally began speaking again.

"She couldn't stay in her condo on Lake Shore Drive. If it had been bigger, maybe I could have found a live-in caregiver, and Mother could have stayed there. But it was too small. Instead of looking for a bigger apartment, I decided to find a place where she'd have constant supervision. Some rehab. Where I hoped she'd recover.

"My first thought was to move her out here, to San Francisco. But the doctors advised against a cross-country move like that. They said she should stay in the area, at least for a while. So I found her a rehab place in Glenview. It seemed nice enough, and the staff promised to take good care of her. I stuck around in Chicago, staying in her condo for a month or so, trying to tie up some loose ends."

Karen nodded.

"While I was there, I made some calls, talked to people at the hospital. Administrators. They didn't want to talk to me. All I wanted was an admission that Andretti and the hospital were responsible for my mother's injuries. But they denied any responsibility. Practically hung up on me.

"Their attitude...it...it made me angry, so I went ahead and got the names of lawyers who represented plaintiffs in cases like this. Maybe one of them would be willing to take Mother's case.

"I wasn't looking for a lot of money. That wasn't what I was after. Just recognition that she'd been harmed, that Andretti and St. Elsa's were responsible. I didn't know much about the law that applied to a case like hers, but I finally connected with a small practice that handled similar cases. One guy, Kevin Robertson, he said he'd take the case."

Karen searched her legal mind, unsure who was legally responsible for injuring Cam's mother. Was it the oaf who knocked her down, or the hospital for allowing the injury to take place on its premises? Or both? Karen's legal experience fell outside the area of personal injury law, so she wasn't really sure.

"Who did you sue?"

"Kevin decided to sue both of them. That bastard Andretti and the hospital. But he screwed up." Cam shook his head in disappointment. "He didn't send out an investigator fast enough to question Andretti before that bastard got himself some lawyers.

"Andretti hired the same big firm that represented the hospital. After that, we couldn't question him until his deposition. By then, his version of events was a complete fabrication. He spouted whatever his sleazy lawyers told him to. 'I wasn't anywhere near her. I couldn't have knocked her down.'" Cam said, mocking a voice he thought sounded like Andretti's. "Anything to avoid taking responsibility for what he'd done."

Karen wondered which law firm had opposed Cam's mother. Sleazy indeed. But she hadn't had any contact with the law firms in Chicago that defended personal injury cases. She probably wouldn't even recognize the name.

"What happened with the lawsuit?" she asked.

Cam's face had brightened a bit when he talked about hiring Kevin Robertson, but now it turned dark again, once more filled with rage.

"It was a disaster, Karen. A total disaster. First, the case against Andretti got thrown out. Kevin later learned the bastard knew the judge, went to her church, something like that. She should have recused herself, but instead she let him off on some pretext or other. The guy was clearly guilty, but Kevin couldn't make it stick."

"And the hospital...?" Karen asked.

"The case against St. Elsa's went forward. I guess the judge couldn't throw it out so fast without looking totally unethical. But the scumbag lawyers representing the hospital forced my mother to give a deposition. Oh, they acted all considerate and caring, holding it at her rehab place, letting me sit in.

"But by then she was so full of the drugs she was getting for her heart condition, she couldn't explain things very clearly. Her mind was fuzzy, and she made a couple of blunders when she tried to answer their questions.

"Kevin was sitting there, but he didn't help very much. Maybe he couldn't. Maybe he had to throw her to the wolves once they demanded that she be deposed."

Karen nodded. It sounded like the defense lawyers were playing hardball all right. "But weren't there any witnesses who could support your mother's side of the story? Hospital staff, other volunteers…?"

"That damned hospital made sure no one on the staff came forward to help my mother. There was one volunteer…another older woman who saw what happened that morning. But the hospital lawyers got to her, too. They must have spent hours with her, undermining her memory of what she saw, until her testimony became pretty shaky. I think Kevin presented it to the trial court, but the judge didn't give it any weight."

"Judge? The case was decided by a judge?"

"Yeah. A judge. A real peach. She granted something called a motion for summary judgment. You probably know what that is."

Karen nodded. So the defense lawyers had filed for summary judgment. If the judge ruled in their favor, that meant the end of the case.

No trial, no jury of her peers, would ever hear his mother's story, her version of the events leading to her injury.

"Right," she said. "I know about summary judgments. So the big firm won?"

"They won, all right. The judge—that miserable bitch—threw out the case. She ruled there was no way my mother could win. That there was insufficient evidence supporting her version of what happened.

"The judge completely disregarded what my mother and the witness had said. So the case was over, just like that. No chance for Mother to tell her story to a jury."

Karen nodded again. That's how summary judgment worked. A lawsuit that might have been successful in front of a jury is dismissed by a judge, fairly or not. It could be devastating to a client like Cam's mother.

"Did you think about appealing the ruling? Going to the appellate court, trying to get the ruling overturned?" A favorable appellate decision would have sent the case back to trial court, ordering the judge to hold a jury trial after all.

Cam looked grim. "Yeah...I discussed it with Kevin. He said he'd appeal, and he did, but I don't think he put his heart into it. I read the brief he filed with the appellate court. I could have written a more convincing brief, Karen.

"He should have played on their heartstrings, talking about this elderly woman and how her life had been ruined by this injury. But the brief he wrote...it was bare-bones legal stuff. Boring as hell. Even judges like to read something livelier than that, don't they?"

"Yes, they do." Karen was well aware how vulnerable judges were to stories that struck a chord with them. A good lawyer, especially a good appellate lawyer, was a good storyteller.

"So the ruling wasn't overturned on appeal?"

"No. No, it wasn't." Cam's face had turned ashen. "We got a 2-to-1 decision. One of the judges dissented. He said the testimony of the only witness should be heard by a jury. But the other two? They were determined to uphold the lower court. Their opinion didn't even bother to spell out any legal basis for the ruling.

"Kevin suspected foul play because one of them was a hospital lawyer before he became a judge. Or maybe some money had changed hands. But the result was those two bastards let the wrongdoers off scot-free."

Karen knew that Cam's negative view of the courts wasn't completely unwarranted. Especially in a city like Chicago, dominated by political hacks-turned-judge.

But still, where was this going?

Cam sighed deeply. "When Mother heard what happened, she was shocked. Disheartened. She'd worked countless hours as a volunteer at that hospital. All she wanted was some recognition of that. Some acknowledgement of how important she was to the hospital. But instead of giving her a few bucks, just as a token, just to show her how much they cared about her, they chose to hand over big bucks to an expensive law firm.

"When I got word of the appellate court decision, I felt sick. Nothing, nothing for my mother, but a big fat fee for that law firm. Was that fair, Karen? Was that fair?"

"No, Cam. I don't think that was fair at all."

"Karen, I sat by my mother's bedside and held her hand. When I told her what happened in court, she cried, saying over and over that the hospital had treated her badly. In my mind's eye, I could just picture the nauseating scene at the law firm. Those bastards were probably celebrating their victory, popping the cork on a pricey bottle of champagne to toast each other and their triumph over a crippled old woman. It made me sick just to think about it."

Karen could see the same picture in her own mind's eye. The lawyers raising glasses of champagne as they saluted each other and the brilliant job they'd done.

What a victory! Depriving an injured old woman of any solace in her last few years.

"It wasn't the money," Cam hastened to assure her. "I have all the money I need, and I had enough to give my mother whatever she needed. It was the principle of the thing. The idea that people who act recklessly and hurt people should take responsibility for their actions. No one should get away with knocking down a fragile elderly woman, especially in a place where she'd gone to help others.

"But Andretti, the hospital--they never admitted their wrongdoing. They never told Mother they'd done anything wrong. They denied any responsibility. And our crooked courts didn't hold them to account."

Cam's face was still filled with rage. What happened to his beloved mother had warped him, made him angry at the world and the way it had hurt her.

Karen couldn't help feeling sympathetic. "Was your mother as angry as you were?"

"Not angry...not angry so much as bitter, Karen. She'd begun to decline anyway, between her weakened heart and the trouble she had walking after the hip surgery. But a positive outcome in her lawsuit might have brightened her life a bit. Being vindicated that way--that would have given her a real lift.

"Instead, she was heartsick, bitter. The nuns and that bastard Andretti had ruined her life, ruined her last few years on this planet. And watching her, so bitter, feeling so betrayed by the hospital, I felt bitter, too. Bitter. And determined to do something about it."

"Do something?"

"Damned right, Karen. I resolved to do something about it."

Cam's face had changed. It had a different cast to it. A look of determination. A look of, well, satisfaction.

What exactly had he done?

Chapter 25

Karen stared at Cam, waiting for him to resume. He picked up his pipe again and this time relighted it. Then he swiveled around in his desk chair, smoking his pipe and gazing at the view outside his windows before he turned toward her to speak.

"Mother lived for one more year after she heard about the appellate court ruling. I'd fly out to Chicago every couple of months to see her at her place in Glenview. I tried to cheer her up, but she declined fast. Her heart finally gave out one morning, and I returned to Chicago to make funeral arrangements.

"A few of her former neighbors, a few friends she'd met over the years, turned up. No one from the hospital, of course. I'd hoped to see Kevin Robertson there, but he was busy. He called the funeral home and left a message for me. There was at least one decent lawyer in Chicago."

Cam's face was grim, even as he said something positive about Kevin Robertson. Karen envisioned the pathetic scene at the funeral home. Cam, waiting there, hoping for mourners who'd seen the obit he'd paid to put in the Chicago papers. But it was a meager turnout, leaving him even angrier than before.

Karen could relate to the immense sadness he felt at losing his mother. Losing her own mother to breast cancer when Karen was in college, losing Jon the way she had—those had been heart-wrenching losses Karen could never forget. Losing her loved ones left her feeling lonely, desolate, sad. But it hadn't made her angry at the world.

Cam had reacted very differently. Losing his mother had stoked even more rage than her original injury. His mother's death had sent him off the deep end.

But what exactly did it lead him to do?

Finally he spoke again. "My first target was Andretti. I had to make him pay for what he did. I decided he would get the punishment he deserved."

"Punishment?"

Cam nodded. "I'd held onto my mother's condo, and I kept going back and forth to Chicago. One day I started to follow Andretti. He'd never seen me, just my mother. I followed him around the city almost every day, careful not to stand out. He frequented a couple of restaurants in the Loop. The Italian Village on Monroe Street, The Berghoff...places like that. Downtown, I'd wear a dark suit and tie with a white dress shirt, looking like all the other men like him in Chicago.

"When he went to the hospital on Thursdays, the day he volunteered, I steered clear, but I followed him to his other favorite haunts--the racetrack a couple of times, a bar in his neighborhood. I'd wear casual clothes there. A polo shirt and khakis. Again, I intentionally didn't stand out, so I don't think he ever noticed me."

Just a regular tall guy, looking like every other tall guy. But this one was stalking his prey.

"All this time, I was trying to come up with a plan. Should I push him in front of an L train? Should I spike his favorite beer with something lethal? I was in a quandary. I'd never done anything like that before, and I wasn't sure what to do."

Cam's face changed. He suddenly looked almost happy, his anger abruptly gone.

"Believe it or not, Karen, my problem was solved at Wrigley Field," he said, smiling.

"Wrigley Field? At a Cubs game?"

"He was alone at a game with the Cardinals, throwing back a few beers. The Cardinals were leading, 6 to nothing, and Andretti was getting pretty worked up. His face was bright red, and he was sweating like crazy. Pretty soon he got up, probably to go to the john after drinking all those beers. I watched him as he walked toward the stairs. The ones that go down to the level with the john.

"As I watched, he stumbled, falling down some stairs. Finally landing on his head. People rushed to help him, but those concrete stairs are killers. I could tell he was seriously injured. A stretcher appeared a few minutes later, and he was carried off. I could hear the ambulance siren above the noise of the crowd.

"I was hoping he was dead. The next morning I saw his obit in the *Tribune*. 'Morris Andretti, retired dentist, dead after a fall at Wrigley Field.'

"Karen, I was delighted. I loved the way things had turned out. The way he died...it was perfect. Just like the way he killed my mother."

"How was that, Cam?" The deaths struck Karen as completely different.

"He fell, Karen. Just like Mother. He fell, and he was the one who caused it to happen. Of course, he died right away, not like Mother. Her death was long and painful. He was spared that pain. So I guess it was only close to perfect. Instead of knocking down my mother, he tripped and knocked himself down. It seemed to me the gods had decided he should die that way, as punishment for killing my mother.

"I left Wrigley Field feeling good. I felt even better the next day, when I read he was dead. Justice had been done, at least in Andretti's case. I watched it happen, and I felt that justice had been done. Do you see what I mean?"

Karen nodded. It was a twisted kind of logic, but Karen could almost understand how Cam felt. An eye for an eye. A fall for a fall.

"That left all the others, Karen."

"The others?"

What is he talking about?

"I had a whole list of targets, Karen. A whole list."

A whole list?

"Unfortunately, I couldn't go after anyone at the hospital. Who could I target from the whole hospital staff? That wasn't a realistic option. So the next one on my list had to be the trial court judge. That stupid bitch, Frieda Hasselhoff."

"The judge?" *His list of targets included the judge?*

Karen's heart began to beat faster.

Was this guy a genuine psycho? A psycho who decided to go after everyone who'd hurt his mother?

"Yes, Karen. The trial court judge, remember? The one who granted the summary judgment that ended Mother's case. So she could never tell her story to a jury."

"I remember, Cam. But when you call her your next target...."

"She was the next one on my list. After Andretti died, I decided to kill them all. I wanted them to pay for what they'd done to my mother."

"K...kill?" Karen had trouble saying the word.

"Yes, kill." He smiled, stroking his salt-and-pepper beard while he went on with his story. "I made a list of all the rotten, miserable people who played a role in destroying my mother's life, and I decided to kill each and every one of them."

Cam pointed to a leather-covered journal sitting on a corner of his desk. "It's all written down in this journal, Karen. Every single name on my list."

"You don't mean...," Karen began. "You don't mean you wanted to kill them...literally kill them. I can understand that you ...."

"Listen to me, Karen," Cam interrupted. "Listen to what I'm saying. I wanted to kill them. Literally kill them, as you put it. And...well, I'll tell you the rest...if you'll shut up and listen."

Karen pulse quickened even more. He was beginning to act aggressively toward her, telling her to shut up.

But I'll play along. I want to hear the rest of his story.

"As I said, Frieda Hasselhoff was the next one on my list. I looked into whether she was still on the court, issuing wretched decisions like the one in Mother's case. What I learned surprised me. A few months after throwing Mother's case out of court, the lovely Frieda had a stroke.

"Not very surprising. She was an enormous woman, 300 pounds, maybe more. All those high-fat meals at chichi restaurants had clogged her arteries, and she had a massive stroke. She was hospitalized for months but never really recovered. By the time I looked into things, she'd died as a result of the stroke. Luckily for me," Cam grinned.

"Luckily?"

"I never had to kill her, Karen. Just like Andretti, she essentially killed herself. In her case, she committed a slow, lengthy suicide, sitting on the bench all day, eating all the wrong food, stuffing her face in between issuing wrong-headed rulings like the one in Mother's case. She got what she deserved. And I didn't have to do a thing." Cam laughed. A short, scoffing laugh.

"You must have been satisfied to see that happen," Karen said. He nodded. "After that, you didn't need to kill anyone else, did you?"

"Are you joking, Karen?" Cam looked at her in disbelief. "I just told you I planned to kill all of them. All of them." He pointed once again at the leather-covered journal.

Karen's head was spinning. "Who...who...?"

"Who was my next target? Actually, there were two of them. The two hacks on the appellate court who'd completely dismissed the travesty in the trial court. But it was hard to choose which one to go after first, Karen."

He smiled again. An awful, twisted smile. "I decided to kill Martin Swanson first. No special reason. Maybe I just liked his name."

"Martin…Martin Swanson?" The name sounded familiar. Karen thought she might have come across one of his rulings during her years as a lawyer in Chicago.

"Good old Martin had retired, as things turned out. And guess where. Out here in California. But not the Bay Area. No, Martin headed for beautiful sunny La Jolla. La Jolla means 'the jewel.' Did you know that, Karen? It really is a jewel. Have you been there?"

Karen had never been anywhere in Southern California. Her growing-up years, her years in school, her life in New York City…those had all been on the East Coast. Then there was her short stay in Wisconsin, followed by the years she spent with Jon and Davi in Chicago and her move to San Francisco just a year ago. No, she hadn't been to La Jolla.

Karen shook her head and waited for Cam to go on.

"Yes, Martin left his comfortable four-bedroom home in Burr Ridge and settled in a condo in La Jolla, where he could play golf from morning till night. Turns out La Jolla has about a dozen golf courses, most of them open to the public. What a deal…." His eyes glazed over. Was he a golf freak himself, envisioning all those opportunities to tee off?

Finally he resumed speaking. "It was easy for me to take care of good old Martin. I flew to San Diego and rented a car, a pretty nondescript one that looked like a million other cars in Southern California. Then I tracked down Martin's condo building in La Jolla, and every time he took off in his neat little BMW, I followed him. I checked out a few of the golf courses where he played and eventually picked one that fit my plan."

138

"Your plan?"

"My plan to kill him, Karen. Haven't you been listening?" A look of annoyance crossed his face. "So I picked a golf course that looked like it would work." Now Cam smiled again, remembering his plan.

"It was a breeze, Karen. I followed Martin into the clubhouse one afternoon. It was a gorgeous day in La Jolla. But then, most days are. I met up with him at the bar. He was knocking back a strong Scotch and soda, and I ordered one, too. We began chatting, and I acted surprised to learn we'd both grown up in Chicago.

"I'd done some research into Martin and learned he was a birder in addition to a golfer. So I said something or other about birds, and that got him going. I made up a lot of bullshit to keep him talking, and at a certain point, I distracted him by telling him I saw a rare bird outside the window near the bar. When he walked over to look at it, I slipped a couple of Xanax tabs into his drink. Xanax plus alcohol will knock someone out. Did you know that?"

Karen shook her head. "No, I didn't. How did you get the Xanax?"

"No problem. I called my internist one day and told him I was feeling especially anxious. He was happy to prescribe Xanax for me, and I picked it up at my friendly neighborhood Walgreens."

"So you were able to knock Martin out that way?"

"Sure. He finished his drink, and a few minutes later, he began to look dizzy. Disoriented. I grabbed his arm and suggested we take a walk outside. He said okay, and we walked out of the clubhouse together. I guided him towards a wooded area surrounding the course. He was getting very wobbly, so I held onto him pretty tight.

"I looked around to make sure no one saw us and dragged him into the trees. Then I pushed him down and smothered him with a sporty cotton square I'd put in my jacket pocket. A big floppy one.

"It was easy, Karen. Easy."

Too easy. Much too easy. "He stopped breathing?"

"Yep. He didn't last very long. Must have had some health issues before I ever got to him. So I probably just pushed him over the edge." Cam suppressed a smile. He seemed pretty damned happy about his success at the La Jolla golf course.

"You left his body there?"

Cam nodded.

"Did anyone ever find him?"

"I guess his wife got worried and eventually contacted the police. She wasn't sure where he'd gone to play golf, so they probably checked all the local golf courses. Finally found his body the next morning, right where I left it. I checked the San Diego papers for a couple of days, and good old Martin's death didn't get much attention. They attributed it to his age and his drinking too much in the clubhouse. I don't think his wife insisted on an autopsy, so they never found the Xanax in his system."

His wife. Karen could imagine the disbelief, the grief his wife felt as a result of Martin's sudden death. *A sudden death like Jon's....*

Karen didn't want to hear any more. She began to rise from the brown velvet sofa.

"You can't go, Karen! You've got to hear the rest of my story!" A menacing look crept over Cam's face. He began to rise from his chair, and Karen feared he would approach her.

She sat back down. "The rest of your story?" Her voice was beginning to tremble.

Cam seated himself again. "I told you I had a whole list of targets, remember? Martin was just the first one. No, actually he was the third one on my list. Andretti and Frieda Hasselhoff had done themselves in, and I took care of Martin in La Jolla. But there were all those others. Remember?"

Karen shuddered.

He keeps talking about his list. This...this list.... It's the stuff of fiction. Agatha Christie in "And Then There Were None." And wasn't there an old movie about a long list of murder victims? Karen thought she'd seen it on late-night TV.

Cam was glaring at her, waiting for her response. But she felt numb, wondering who he targeted next.

He seemed to read her mind. "You're wondering who was next. Right?" This time he didn't even wait for a nod from Karen before he continued.

"Did you forget there was another judge who ruled against my mother? Another judge so eager to help the bad guys, so eager to throw out Mother's case...? Well, I didn't forget. I didn't forget the bastard Charlie Santini. A charming product of Chicago's North Side.

"Killing him posed more problems than bumping off Martin Swanson, but I was up to the challenge." Cam smiled outright now, not bothering to suppress his glee.

Oh, my God. He really is deranged. Karen felt shaky, breathless.

How can I get out of here? I have to get out of here. Her eye fell once again on the artwork leaning against the wall. *I'll mention the artwork....*

Before Karen could catch her breath, Cam cheerfully launched into his story again. "I did some research on Charlie Santini and discovered he was a diabetic. A grossly overweight diabetic. Type 2 and dependent on insulin. That sent me to the internet to read about diabetes and the diabetics who need insulin. It took a while, but I finally found something. If you add gatifloxican to insulin, you can create havoc with a diabetic's medical condition, maybe even cause a heart attack. The heart attack would appear to be routine. The cause—the gatifloxican—would most likely be undetectable."

Now a wave of nausea hit Karen. *Killing Santini this way? Again, it was much too easy.*

"But it wasn't as easy as it sounds." Cam had read her mind again. "I had to get access somehow to Charlie's insulin and add the gatifloxican without anyone noticing."

"What is...gatiflox...?"

"Gatifloxican. It's an antibiotic used as drops to treat eye infections. While I was back in San Francisco, I got some by calling my ophthalmologist and telling her I had a bad eye infection. She wanted to see me before prescribing anything, but I told her I was in Palo Alto and couldn't see her right away. When she hesitated, I added that my friend had used these drops and they cured his infection right away. She was reluctant to do it, but she finally called in a prescription to a pharmacy in Palo Alto. I picked them up just before going to Chicago."

Karen stared at Cam, waiting....

"You're wondering how I did it, right? Well, once I was back in Chicago, I followed Charlie around for a week or two. He was still sitting on the appeals court, dispensing injustice right and left. The court was hearing oral arguments in its courtroom in the Daley Center almost every morning, but I avoided going to the courtroom. I didn't want to be noticed by people like the bailiff and the law clerks.

"After I hung around the Daley Center for a while, I realized that Charlie would go to his chambers every afternoon. Unless one of his law clerks came by, he was alone. He apparently sat at his desk and fiddled around till he could leave for home at a respectable hour, looking like he'd put in a full day's work.

"I wasn't sure he'd keep his insulin supply anywhere near his chambers, but one day I sneaked into the kitchen on his floor and took a look in the fridge. There it was, right in front of me. A box with a few vials of insulin sitting on the top shelf. Charlie's name was on the printout from the pharmacy where he bought it, so I knew it was his.

"I couldn't count on being able to get into that kitchen again so easily, so I'd wisely brought along a syringe filled with gatifloxican drops. I had a lot of it, enough for three vials of insulin, and I injected it into the vials, using my syringe."

Once again, Cam smiled, pleased with his competence as a killer. Then he went on with his horrific story.

"A law clerk, one working for a different judge, entered just after I finished. 'Can I help you?' she asked. She looked uneasy, and I had to come up with something. Luckily, I'd thought of a cover story in case anyone saw me. 'Oh, Judge Anderson asked me to look for her yogurt,' I said, smiling to make everything seem okay. 'Judge Anderson?' she said, looking dubious.

"'She's from the Third District, just filling in here while someone's on vacation,' I added. She still looked skeptical but finally poured herself a cup of coffee from the coffeemaker on the counter and left."

"What happened to Santini?" Karen held her breath.

"I stayed in Chicago a few days to find out. I wasn't sure the gatifloxican had worked. I had a backup plan, of course, in case it didn't. But two days after my visit to the Daley Center, TV news and the papers covered Santini's sudden death from an apparent heart attack. No one seemed suspicious that his death resulted from anything other than natural causes. The guy was an overweight diabetic, and a death like his happens all the time."

"So you pulled off another one...."

"Yes, indeed. That's exactly what I did." Cam beamed, looking extremely satisfied.

Karen thought once again of the pain he'd caused. The pain felt by Santini's wife, his children.

Another sudden death like Jon's. Only this one was caused by a madman.

"I have to leave now, Cam," she said plaintively. "I don't feel very good."

"No," he said. The menacing look had returned. "You can't leave, Karen. You have to hear the rest of the story."

Karen felt a strong urge to vomit. The room seemed to be moving, and she felt dizzy.

"Please, Cam. I don't think I can hear any more...."

Chapter 26

"I don't think I can hear any more...," Karen repeated, her voice even shakier than before.

Cam's story had begun to remind Karen of similar stories. Stories of other men who'd sought to kill targets on a list. While she was working in Chicago, she'd heard some 1920s gangland lore: Al Capone had reputedly made a list to avenge his brother's murder.

More recently she'd learned about the Israeli government's plot to track down and kill the men who massacred Israeli athletes during the Munich Olympics. The government had come up with a list of the murderers. Spielberg was making a film about it.

Maybe stories like Cam's aren't pure fiction after all.

"But Karen," Cam said, "I'm getting to the best part. The judges were just practice for me. They were fucking bastards, of course. They completely disregarded the merits of my mother's case. But my real targets...."

He paused, watching for Karen's reaction. She tried not to show any.

"My real targets, as I'm sure you've guessed, were the lawyers. The lawyers who fought tooth and nail to triumph over my mother. They were the...."

"But Cam...." Karen knew she should keep quiet, let Cam finish talking. But she couldn't stop herself. "Lawyers do nothing more than represent their clients. Yes, they sometimes represent bad guys, but they themselves aren't the bad guys. Why target them?"

"Karen, Karen, I understand what you're saying. As a lawyer, you see things from the lawyer's point of view. But when lawyers represent bad guys, as you call them, I view *them* as bad guys, too. Lawyers don't have to go to bat for every client who walks in the door. They can choose who they help.

"The lawyers who decided to demolish my mother's case…they did it for the money or for a pat on the back from some muckety-muck hospital administrator. Maybe they just liked the idea of depriving an old woman of getting what was owed to her. Depriving her of an ounce of compensation for all the pain and hardship she endured.

"They could have thrown her a bone, you know. Admit some responsibility and cough up a few of the hospital's bucks, just to give her some satisfaction. But no, these lawyers wanted to destroy her, leave her with nothing, glory in their victory on behalf of those who'd wronged her."

His angry face was back, but this time the anger was mixed with sadness. His eyes glazed over, and it seemed to Karen he was reliving the hours he sat by his mother's bedside, listening to the bitterness erupting from the woman he loved so much.

"So," he said, "after succeeding so brilliantly with the fucking judges—first, good old Martin and then fat Charlie Santini, I decided to move on to the lawyers. I thought at first about going after Kevin Robertson. He'd done a lousy job as Mother's lawyer. But I had to admit he'd tried to help her. He meant well. So I decided to leave him be.

"The lawyers on the other side…hey, Karen, you were a lawyer in Chicago, maybe you knew some of them. There were three bastards I targeted. Let's see…."

Karen waited. It was indeed possible that she might have known one of Cam's targets. She hadn't known many lawyers who defended personal injury cases, but there was always a chance….

"The first one I went after was Arthur O'Connor. A big deal lawyer in Chicago."

Karen's heart skipped a beat. *That name sounds familiar. Why?*

"Oh, yes, Arthur O'Connor. Good old Artie. His name came first on all the legal documents filed in Mother's case. So I checked him out. He was one of the oldest guys in his firm. Not very active anymore. Described on the firm website as 'of counsel,' whatever that means."

Karen knew what it meant. It usually described older lawyers who no longer played a major role at their firms.

"When I watched Artie leave his office building on LaSalle Street for lunch at his private club," Cam continued, "he seemed unsteady on his feet. After a two-drink lunch, he was even more unsteady.

"After watching him for a week or two, I followed him one afternoon as he walked back to his office. When he got to a busy intersection—Clark and Madison—I sidled up to him. Karen, it was so easy! We stood there next to each other, waiting for the light to change, and when a small truck approached us, I gave him a push. He fell into the street, right in front of the truck. People saw him fall, but no one saw me push him. I turned and began to walk back slowly through the crowd. While people began to yell for help, I just kept walking.

"His death was reported that afternoon on TV news. Witnesses said he'd apparently stumbled and fell in front of the truck. He'd died instantly. I'd succeeded with him so fast, and so easily, I could scarcely believe my luck. Shouldn't it have been harder?"

Karen's head was spinning. Arthur O'Connor, a lawyer whose name sounded familiar, killed by a truck on the streets of Chicago an instant after Cam pushed him.

Another wife, children, maybe even grandchildren, left to deal with his loss.

Karen felt dehydrated, her mouth dry as parchment. "Cam, I need something to drink. Can I get a glass of water?"

He scanned her face and apparently decided she was telling the truth. "Okay. You can have some water. But I'll get it."

He grudgingly rose from his desk chair and moved toward the doorway. Turning back toward Karen, he warned her, "Now don't move. I'll be right back. I want you to hear the rest of the story. You need to hear it."

Need to hear the rest of the story? Why? Karen's heart began racing again. Why did she "need" to hear the rest of the story?

Watching Cam leave the room, Karen grabbed her handbag and searched for her cell phone. Her heart sank. *I must have left it on the desk in my office when I ran out to come here.*

Now what? Karen breathlessly considered whether she had a realistic chance to escape Cam's clutches. She had begun to hear echoes of her confrontation with a madman in Walden, Wisconsin: another psycho driven by his demons to kill.

I don't want to hear any more. If I get up right now, I can run out of the house, call the police. If he tries to stop me, I can...I can use tae kwan do....

Cam returned before she could. He was carrying a glass filled with water for Karen and a shot glass filled with amber-colored liquid for himself.

Scotch? Karen couldn't be sure. He threw back the amber liquid while Karen scrutinized the glass of water he'd brought her.

He wouldn't have put something in the water, would he? She paused. *No, he wants me to hear his story. He wants my head to be clear so I can fully comprehend what he's telling me.*

She put caution aside and thirstily gulped down some of the water in the glass.

"Okay," Cam said, "we'll move on to Lawyer #2. Arnold Kucher. Ring a bell?"

Karen felt her stomach lurch. She dropped the glass she'd been holding, spilling what remained of the water on Cam's beige carpeting.

Arnold Kucher? I knew Arnold Kucher. I worked with him at Stein & Walter right after I started there.

True, she hadn't seen much of him—their areas of law didn't intersect—but as a new associate, she'd been pulled into preparing one or two memoranda for him.

Cam was grinning now. "So his name rings a bell, huh? You knew this guy in Chicago, right?"

Karen nodded, trying to stay calm. "Just tell me what happened to Arnold."

"I decided it was time for another heart attack. That ploy at the busy intersection in downtown Chicago—I couldn't hope to get away with that again. So I had to be creative with Arnold. Once more I delved into medical research, and this time I discovered a substance called sodium fluoroacetate. It can cause a heart attack.

"I had a little problem, though. Arnold was in good shape for 62. He worked out at the Westlake Club twice a week—Tuesday and Friday mornings--before going to work. But according to my research, plenty of lawyers have unexpected heart attacks, and I decided that Arnold would become one of them. A heart attack in a lawyer in his 60s, even one in pretty good shape, wouldn't be totally unheard of."

"How, how...d...did you do it?" Karen tried to keep her voice steady.

"I used sodium fluoroacetate." Cam looked pleased as punch to explain how he'd killed Arnold Kucher.

Karen just stared at him, unable to believe what he was saying.

"I used sodium fluoroacetate, Karen. It's a salt, like sodium chloride. Colorless and tastes like ordinary table salt. But it's a poison, a pretty scary poison. So scary it's tightly controlled in this country. Only one company still makes it, a chemical company in Alabama, and they use it in the U.S. to kill coyotes. Coyotes!"

"How were you able to get it?

"This company in Alabama exports it to Mexico and a couple of other countries. They still use it there as rat poison. So I hopped on a plane to Mexico City. I didn't even have to stay overnight. I took a taxi from the airport to a busy part of town and walked into a storefront pharmacy. There are plenty of pharmacies like that all over Mexico. When I said I was having a problem with rats, the guy at the counter was happy to get a few different kinds of rat poison from the back. One of them was sodium fluoroacetate. I paid for it, and he handed it to me. With a smile."

Karen shook her head. Another means to kill someone, obtainable so easily. One short flight to Mexico City, and Cam had the poison. *But once he had it, what then?*

"What did you do? Did you put it in his food?"

"That's exactly what I did." He beamed as he began to relate how clever he'd been. "One Monday morning, I dropped in at the Westlake Club. When I inquired about membership, the staff was delighted to give me a one-week pass to try it out. I came back the next morning at 6 a.m. and caught a glimpse of Arnold working out.

"When Arnold went into the locker room to change, I followed him. Asked if he was Arnold Kucher and did he know Asa Stein. I'd picked the name of one of the firm's founding lawyers from the website. I figured Arnold would know him, and of course he did.

"I wanted him to think I knew this guy, so I told him I'd met Asa at a party. I added that when I told Asa I was planning to move to Chicago, he said I should try to meet up with Arnold at the club.

"Arnold nodded and shook my hand. Then I asked him if he wanted to get a bite to eat. 'My treat,' I said. He looked at his watch and finally said, 'What the hell.'

"I looked around to make sure no one was watching us as we entered the coffee bar. It wasn't crowded, and I picked a table in a far corner. I was wearing a Cubs baseball hat, like half the people in Chicago, and it obscured my features pretty well. Arnold seemed interested to learn that I was still living in San Francisco, and he asked a lot of questions about life out here.

"I ordered scrambled eggs for both of us, and when he looked away to say hello to someone, I added the sodium fluoroacetate to his eggs. He must have been hungry because he wolfed them down.

"After he polished off the eggs, we said goodbye, and I went on my merry way. I wasn't sure the poison would work, but I knew that if it did, it would happen fairly soon. According to what I read on the internet, symptoms of poisoning appear in an hour or two. The symptoms can be life-threatening, like an abnormally fast heart rate. Death is usually due to 'ventricular arrhythmias.'"

Cam used air quote marks around the last two words. He didn't seem to have a clear understanding of what they meant.

Karen didn't know what they meant either. She wondered for a moment whether the same thing had led to Jon's death. She'd never really wanted to know the technical details of what had killed him. What difference did it make?

"So...so...what...happened to Arnold?" Karen asked, her voice shaky.

"I hung around Chicago for a few more days to find out. By the third day, there was a small obit in the *Tribune*: 'Prominent lawyer dies of heart attack.' The story said Arnold regularly worked out at the Westlake Club, where fellow club members were shocked by his sudden death. It was attributed to large quantities of caffeine, possibly exacerbated by large quantities of alcohol."

"But Arnold wasn't known to be a big drinker," Karen said, easily recalling the names of some of the lawyers at Stein & Walter who were.

"Maybe he was and maybe he wasn't. But I'm sure he drank a lot of coffee. Most lawyers do, don't they, Karen?" Cam smiled malevolently. "And he might have been hooked on cocaine. That can be harmful to the heart. Don't some lawyers use cocaine?"

"I don't know, Cam. I suppose some of them do."

"Well, Arnold's death must have shaken up a lot of people at the Westlake Club. People who thought regular exercise insulated them from heart problems." Cam snorted, delighted that his murdering Arnold had made a whole lot of people, especially lawyers, fearful about their health.

Karen tried to resurrect what she knew about Arnold Kucher. She recalled hearing that he'd died a sudden death; she'd overheard some office chatter about it. But she hadn't had any contact with Arnold for years, and she was too preoccupied with her own life at that point to focus on what had happened to him.

He must have died when I was busy getting ready to move here. Overwhelmed, really. No time to think about Arnold Kucher.

"I tracked Arnold's name on the internet for a while," Cam continued. "Despite the suddenness of his death, his family apparently didn't request an autopsy. Maybe they suspected something like cocaine and didn't want that revealed. So, without an autopsy, the sodium fluoroacetate was never detected."

Cam grinned. Another easily accomplished death he could chalk up. Another target on his list eliminated.

"Now, let's see," he continued. "Who was next on my list? I need to think for a minute...." His eyes narrowed, carefully watching Karen.

Her pulse quickened. She suspected that he was about to spring another name on her, this time one she knew well.

"I don't suppose you knew Harold McBeth, did you?" Cam said.

Harold! Karen's heart began racing. Of course she knew Harold! She'd worked closely with him her first six months at Stein & Walter. His specialty was tort defense work, and he usually defended big corporations, like manufacturers and retailers accused of injuries on their premises. Karen remembered writing a couple of memoranda for him before she began to focus on estate-planning.

"You worked with him, didn't you?" Cam's malevolent smile had returned.

It's pretty clear now. I helped Harold with a couple of his cases. One of them must have been Cam's mother's case.

"Yes, I worked with Harold. Did I...did I help him defend the people who...who were responsible for what happened to your mother?"

"Bingo!" Cam's face registered a variety of emotions. At first, he kept smiling. Then, his eyes narrowing again, rage took over. Suddenly rage was itself replaced by joy. Joy at Karen's discovery, at long last realizing that she'd played a part—albeit a very small part—in the decline leading to the bitterness-filled death of his beloved mother.

Karen buried her face in her hands. *Another death. Another lawyer, doing his job, killed by a rage-driven maniac seeking revenge.*

Karen finally looked up at Cam. She was calmer now. "How did you kill Harold?"

She knew she was herself in danger, but she had to stay calm, keep cool, to hear more of Cam's demented story.

"Harold was quite a challenge for me, Karen. I did a thorough background check, of course. Followed him, too. The guy didn't drink or do drugs, and he didn't like coffee. Didn't play golf and didn't work out at a gym. Went home every night to his wife and kids in Glencoe. Churchgoer, and a big donor to the local Republican party. In short, a good family man with no vices. So I had a hard time figuring out what to do.

"But he was my primary target, Karen. He was the lead lawyer opposing Mother. So I kept looking...."

Karen waited.

"Then one day, he didn't show up at work. I figured he had something like a bad cold, decided to stay home that day. But when he didn't show up the next day, I looked up his phone number at the firm. I used a pay phone—a few of those are still around—and talked to his assistant. She was reluctant to say anything, but I told her I was a college classmate from out of town hoping to get in touch with him. Could she tell me where he was?

"Finally, she came out with it. Our pal Harold was in San Francisco, attending a legal conference.

"Convenient for me, huh, Karen? I flew back here and tried to track down all the legal conferences in town. But that week there was only one. A conference for IP lawyers. I knew Harold never touched intellectual property, so that couldn't be where he was. Maybe he was kicking back. Just being a tourist here. I began looking for him at some of our famous tourist sites—Coit Tower, Fisherman's Wharf, the Japanese Garden in Golden Gate Park. Every place was packed with tourists, but I never saw Harold.

"I was beginning to think of giving up. Then I had a hunch. Maybe Mr. Perfect wasn't as upright as he wanted everyone to think. Maybe he liked to follow a different lifestyle when he went out of town. So I hit some of the most popular bars in town, including a few of the gay bars. And that's where I found him. In a gay bar in the Castro. Dressed rather colorfully for a conservative lawyer from the Midwest. Drinking a lot, too. A total departure from the persona he projected in Chicago."

Karen's eyes widened. Harold McBeth at a gay bar? Drinking a lot? And colorfully dressed? That certainly didn't jibe with the Harold she'd known.

"Once I tracked him down in that bar, the rest was easy. I'd paid a guy outside one of the bars in the Mission to give me some roofies. You know what roofies are?"

Karen nodded.

"People like to call them 'date rape drugs,' and I'm sure you know why. The most popular one is Rohypnol, but they actually come in all shapes and sizes. This guy in the Mission offered me a variety to choose from, but he especially pushed one he called Liquid X. I later found out it was liquid ecstasy, sometimes called GHB. In small doses, it makes people feel euphoric, uninhibited. The kids involved in the bar scene love it. But in large doses, it has a powerful effect on the heart rate.

"The dealer told me not to use too much because an overdose can kill somebody. Little did he know, that's exactly what I wanted.

"I had no trouble buddying up to Harold in the bar. He was happy to talk to me. Began pouring out his angst with life as a lawyer in Chicago. Actually told me he hated having to represent 'bad actors' who hurt 'the little guy.' But Karen, that's precisely what he did. Making a bundle to support his lavish lifestyle in Glencoe. He chose that life, didn't he, Karen? Nobody made him do it. Right?"

Karen nodded again. She was revolted by everything he'd been saying, but she felt compelled to sit there and hear the rest of his story.

I have to know. I have to know how he killed Harold...and got away with it.

"He called himself 'Hal,' by the way. 'Hal King.' King Macbeth, get it? He was drinking rum and cokes. When he looked away for a moment and I slipped a big dose of GHB into his drink, I knew he'd never notice it.

"After he chugged it down, I made my excuses and told him I had to run. We said goodbye, and I took off, grabbing a Muni bus—the 24—so I wouldn't have a cab driver who could identify me."

"Harold died that night, didn't he, Cam?"

"He did. Maybe you heard about it?"

"I did. I'd just moved here. I was reading the *Chronicle* every day, trying to learn as much as I could about San Francisco, and I came across a short piece about Harold's death. I was shocked that a lawyer I knew in Chicago had been found dead under suspicious circumstances in the Castro. But it didn't give any details."

"I saw the story, too," Cam said. "You're right, there were no details. But somehow the police were able to identify him. When I looked online a few days later, I learned his body was found in a parking lot near the Castro Theater. Someone working at the bar must have dragged it there, hoping the bar wouldn't be implicated. The police couldn't track down anyone who remembered seeing him at a bar in the Castro. The bars were all crowded, and many of their patrons looked a lot like him."

Cam stopped to think for a minute. Then he spoke again. "The GHB really polished Harold off fast. It's a dangerous drug, Karen. You know, when your daughter's older, you'd better warn her to stay away from guys who'd try to put it in her drinks..."

"My daughter? Davi...?" Karen stared at Cam. *How could he? How could this monster pretend to have any concern for Davi?*

Cam turned to view the bay through his windows, and Karen glanced around the room, trying to think up a pretext—a pretext enabling her to run out the door before he could overpower her. Her gaze fell on Cam's framed artwork, some of which was leaning against a wall, unhung.

Karen suddenly glimpsed something that looked vaguely familiar. One of the unhung items wasn't really artwork at all. It looked like a diploma. Only part of the diploma was visible, most of it hidden behind the assorted frames and other items covering the floor, but Karen recognized it.

It was a framed Harvard diploma. Karen had one like it from the law school. She kept it on a closet shelf in her bedroom, planning to bring it downtown someday to hang on her office wall.

She wondered why a diploma would be sitting on the floor like that. While Cam turned away from his windows and began relighting his pipe, she tried to scrutinize the diploma more closely.

She could, with difficulty, make out a few letters. She squinted, trying to decipher them. The letters on the top line, the few that could be read despite all the other stuff surrounding the diploma…were they part of the word "HARVARDIANA"?

The way Harvard's Latin name also appeared on her diploma.

Were they…could they possibly be…"DIANA"?

And the letters that appeared just below that? What were they?

Were they part of Cam's name?

She searched her brain, trying to remember his full name.

It finally popped into her consciousness: Cameron Meredith Harper. Wasn't that it?

The few legible letters on that line of the diploma—the line where the graduate's name appeared—spelled out..."RED."

The middle letters in his middle name. "RED."

DIANA. RED. DIANA. RED DIANA...RED DIANA.

Karen's heart stopped. She thought she might faint.

The only legible letters on the framed diploma spelled out "Red Diana." The words Davi remembered.

The words burned into Davi's brain.

So Cam had grabbed Davi and forced her to stay in this house, in this room.

Why? Why?

I think I know.

He did it to get at me....

Chapter 27

Karen took a deep breath and tried to compose herself. It was time to confront Cam Harper. Time to say something, time to do something. Time to run out the door if she had to.

"You kidnapped Davi, didn't you?"

There, she'd said it. She'd said the word "kidnap." She didn't really know the legal distinction between a "kidnapping" and an "abduction," but "kidnapping" sounded so much worse.

Karen thought he'd flinch when she accused him of kidnapping. But he didn't. "Did you kidnap Davi to punish me? Was I your next target?"

Cam looked almost amused. "Gee, Karen, I knew you were smart. I knew you'd figure things out if I gave you enough to go on," he said, smiling.

"You're right," he went on. "You were my next target." He stroked his well-groomed beard again, enhancing the malevolence of his smile.

"Then why didn't you just go ahead and kill me, Cam? Why did you go after my daughter?"

Tell me why! I deserve to know....

Cam paused, awkwardly relighting his pipe again before looking up to face Karen. "You were a special case, Karen. A special case. I can't put it any other way. I found your name at the very bottom of a list of lawyers' names on one document filed in Mother's case. Only one document, and at the bottom of the list. I figured you were a new addition to the firm and hauled in to do some last-minute research for the partners. Was I right?"

Karen nodded emphatically. "I don't even remember working on your mother's case. I was new at the firm, and whenever a partner said 'Jump,' I jumped. I did the partners' bidding whether I liked it or not.

"Please believe me, Cam, I never wanted to do that kind of work. It disgusted me. It reminded me of the work I'd done at a big firm in New York, a firm I hated. I practically begged them to let me move into another field.

"After the first few months, after I proved I was an asset to the firm, the partners agreed to let me do the kind of work I wanted to do. So I was never forced to work on another case like your mother's." Karen paused. "And I'm very glad I wasn't."

Cam was silent, just staring at Karen, so she kept going. "Please believe me," she repeated, "I never wanted to help the bad guys in your mother's case. I had to do it to keep my job. I was a new hire, and the partners could have seized on my refusal to work on it and let me go."

Again he was silent.

"Even if you thought I was as bad as the other lawyers in the case," Karen continued, "even if you wanted to hurt me, why did you go after Davi? Why did you grab her and keep her in this room for so many hours?"

After a long pause, Cam finally answered. "I did want to hurt you. You were in the cast of characters who destroyed my mother's life. But in fairness, I had to admit you played a minor role.

"I don't know much about the law, but it was pretty clear to me that you weren't one of the truly bad guys. One of those lawyers who fought my mother tooth and nail. Using any legal means they could to deprive Mother of the tiny bit of satisfaction she might have otherwise gotten from Andretti and the hospital.

"You...you were different. It seemed to me you were plucked from the ranks to research some little tidbit of the law that would bolster their case in some way."

Karen nodded. "So then why...?"

"Why?" Cam repeated. "Truthfully, I agonized over what to do about you. I really did. Once I learned you'd moved to San Francisco, I decided to follow you around the city. I thought that if I followed you, maybe I'd come up with a plan. But I really had no idea what to do."

"You followed me?"

"Yes. I did. You never noticed, did you?"

Karen shook her head.

"You'd started working at that small law firm downtown...that was easy to find out. When I met you at the opera, you confirmed it. I also discovered you were living not too far from here. Great location, isn't it?"

A bizarre question in the middle of his confession. Karen blinked, startled by how bizarre it was. But she decided to nod again, just to keep him talking.

"It was a breeze to follow you, Karen. But I still didn't know what to do. And then...then I saw you with a little girl. A very cute little girl....
"

Karen's heart skipped a beat. Finally, he would say something about Davi.

"You watched her pretty closely, Karen. That created a real problem for me."

"A problem? What kind of problem?"

"All the other lawyers on my list, the judges, even Andretti...they were all much older than you. Even if they had kids, their kids were grown. When I tracked those guys, I never saw any little kids, so I never had to worry about that. Never had to decide how to handle the problem of a little kid. But you...you had one around all the time.

"If I was going to go after you somehow, I needed to get you alone. Sidle up to you at a bar, put something in your drink. But you never went to any bars alone, did you? You went out for a drink with some people at your firm once or twice. But you stayed with the group. And you wouldn't stay very long, always rushing to get back home."

That's right. I did. I rushed back home to be with Davi.

"There were other problems," Cam continued. "As far as I could tell, you were in perfect health. No way to tamper with any meds, insulin, that kind of thing. You also seemed to be busy at work, surrounded by your colleagues, or busy taking your daughter back and forth to school. And she was always closely supervised at that school.

"But things changed last summer. Things finally changed. The school year was over, and pretty soon I noticed that your daughter was taking a bus to day camp every day. I kept watching you, and I kept watching her, and I waited for something to happen. Some opening for me to get to you. And then I found it."

Karen felt a wave of nausea wash over her. Just as she'd always known, it was her fault. Her fault that this psycho was able to get to Davi.

My fault that I let Davi come downtown. My fault that I let Davi go downstairs to get some M&M's.

"Day camp must have ended because one day the bus didn't show up at your building anymore. Your daughter suddenly had an erratic schedule, going to a friend's home one day, staying in your apartment with a babysitter another day. It seemed to be impossible for me to grab you, so I pondered my options. Wait for your daughter to be alone in the apartment? Or watch her when she'd be somewhere else, somewhere I could grab her?

"As you know, Karen, the day finally arrived. The day I followed the two of you downtown. That morning you walked to Union Street together and took the 45 bus downtown. I followed the bus in my car and double-parked near your office building. I waited outside, drinking lattes from Starbucks, trying to decide what to do. I was wearing a Giants baseball cap, hoping it would obscure my features the way the Cubs cap had.

"I wasn't as prepared as I'd been with my other targets. Everything had been up in the air with you for months, and all I'd done was bring along a bandana to cover her eyes. Nothing else.

"I was stupid not to be better prepared."

Better prepared? Better prepared to kidnap a child? How monstrous. How quintessentially evil.

Karen was finding it hard to breathe. She forced herself to take another breath and keep listening.

"Then I saw your daughter leaving your office building all by herself. I admit it, I was shocked. For once, no Karen hovering over her. She went into the 7-Eleven near your building. I knew I had to move quickly, so I ran toward the door and grabbed her from behind when she left the store. She was so startled she didn't make a sound. Luckily for me." A smile crossed his face. Again, he'd been so very lucky.

"I told her everything was OK, that her mother wanted me to take her somewhere. That her mother would be angry with her if she gave me any trouble. She struggled a little to get free, dropping a package of candy she'd been clutching, but I kept my arms tightly around her from behind. When we got to my car, I put the bandana over her eyes and pushed her into the back seat. She never saw my face."

Karen tried to imagine the terror her small daughter must have felt. She hoped that Davi didn't completely understand what was happening to her.

"We got back here, and I stashed her in this room and locked the door while I found a Halloween mask I'd once bought on Fillmore Street. When I put it on, I could tell that it covered most of my face. Then I came back to the room and removed her bandana. I told her she'd be okay, her mother would be here soon, and I gave her a Coke and some stale cookies I had in the kitchen. What do you feed a kid like that?"

Karen stared impassively at him. *Does he really care what I feed her? Of course not.*

"I had no idea what to feed a kid, but I hoped the cookies would fill her up."

Sure. Less trouble for him if they did.

"Oh, yeah," he continued, "I added something to her Coke. I had some Ambien in the kitchen, so I mashed one up and put a little bit in her Coke, hoping she would fall asleep."

Ambien? He gave Ambien to Davi? She's so small, he could have given her an overdose!

Thankfully, he didn't. Just enough to knock her out for a while. So she could sleep through the rest of her terrible ordeal.

Cam glibly went on with his story. "I locked her in the room again and started thinking. I really hadn't given much thought to any of it. I didn't have a plan, but now I had to come up with one. I needed some way to contact you, to get back at you for your work on Mother's case. I was up all night, trying to decide what to do."

***You** were up all night? You monster....*

"Finally I decided to write that note, pin it on her shirt, and drive her somewhere. A place where no one would notice her right away. I woke her up and told her I was taking her someplace where her mom would pick her up. She was still groggy from the Ambien, but I was able to get her downstairs and into my car without any trouble. I put the bandana over her eyes again so she wouldn't see exactly where I was going.

"I drove around for a while till I found that parking lot. I helped her out of the car and told her you'd pick her up in a few minutes. Then I called your office from a pay phone on the corner and told you where to find her.

"After that, I came back here, not sure what would happen next."

Karen gathered her strength. Her heart was pounding, but she had to ask the question that had been plaguing her. "Why did you pin that note on her shirt? The note that said 'You're next, Karen.' Why did you do that? You'd already terrified both my daughter and me. But why did you write that note? Why?"

Cam paused. Then he spoke again. "I wanted to make you suffer, Karen. Everything I did--grabbing your daughter...keeping her here overnight...putting that note on her shirt. I figured it would make you suffer for what you did at that law firm."

"Well, you succeeded, Cam. You made me into a basket case."

"But I didn't harm her in any way. You told me that at the restaurant. You found her in the parking lot, and she wasn't hurt, right?"

Karen found it hard to stay calm and keep talking to Cam. But she was determined to make him understand the consequences of what he'd done. "That's right," she began, her voice shaking, "you didn't harm her physically. And I'm grateful for that. But you don't seem to have any idea what you've done to her, let alone to me."

Cam looked away, gazing through his windows again. He was silent.

He's lived with his anger and his desire for revenge all these years. It's been festering in his brain for a very long time.

But I need to get through to him. Let him know just how wrong his actions were.

"Cam," she began, "you've told me how much your mother meant to you. You wanted to take your revenge on everyone who caused her so much pain. But do you realize how much pain you've caused my eight-year-old daughter? You traumatized an innocent child. Thank God, a therapist has helped her deal with that trauma, but you seriously damaged my precious daughter."

Cam slowly turned back to Karen. His face had changed. *He feels defensive now. He wants to defend himself, defend what he's done.*

"You're wrong, Karen, to talk about revenge," he said sharply. "I wasn't seeking revenge. I was seeking *justice*. Justice for my beloved mother, who didn't deserve what happened to her.

"Justice for me, too, for the pain I've suffered. Losing my mother, watching her suffer. Being treated so unfairly by the crooked judges and the unethical lawyers. I wanted justice, Karen. <u>Justice</u>."

Karen paused before going on. It was clear now. He had vowed to avenge his mother's death. But Karen needed to say her piece.

I have to confront him. Now.

"You speak so lovingly of your mother, Cam. She must have loved you, too. The way I love my daughter, and the way that she loves me. The love between Davi and me is boundless. You and your mother...you must have felt the same way.

"But, Cam, didn't she raise you to be a good man? A man who cares about others? Do you think she would have approved of what you've done? Playing God with other people's lives the way you have?

"Sure," Karen continued, "there's some truth to what you say about the courts. Some judges are corrupt or stupid...or both. And yes, I agree that some lawyers are unethical. They try to demolish their opponents regardless of the merits of a case. The law is a game to lawyers like that.

They lose sight of the human cost, the damage done to people in cases like your mother's.

"But that's not a good enough reason to kill people, Cam. Or to kidnap an innocent child. It just isn't."

Cam was silent. He looked down at his desktop and remained silent for a very long time.

Say something! Admit that you're a monster!

When he finally spoke again, he no longer seemed defiant. No longer insistent that he'd been seeking nothing more than justice. His face, his whole demeanor had changed. He now looked sad, even remorseful.

Does he see, at last, that what he's done was wrong?

"I understand what you're saying, Karen. I wasn't thinking clearly, I see that now.

"I <u>was</u> wrong...I was wrong to target you and your daughter. You...you'd played such a small role in my mother's case. And your daughter...she was completely innocent. I was wrong, Karen. I was wrong..."

At last...at last he admits that he was wrong.

Karen's breathing began to return to normal. She could leave now. Cam wouldn't try to stop her.

Just then Cam pulled open the bottom drawer in his desk and reached into it. His hands were shaking as he took out a small handgun and stared at it.

A gun! What is he doing, pulling out a gun?

He looked back at Karen. His face had turned ashen.

"Now that you know the whole story, Karen, what am I going to do with you? You can go to the police, tell them everything. And you have every right to do that. I've ruined your life and your daughter's...and now all three of us will have nothing but misery for the rest of our lives."

"Wait a minute, Cam." Karen spoke quickly, terrified by what he might do. "I don't plan to go to the police. Look, I understand why you did what you did. The desire for revenge, the desire for justice. It's a perfectly normal human emotion. We all want vengeance against those who've hurt us, hurt our loved ones."

I have to reach him—with words if nothing else—before he points the gun at me.

"I'm angry with you, sure, but what's important is you now realize you were wrong," she said. "That's enough for me.

"I don't want to see you get in trouble, Cam. I really don't. Those lawyers you killed. The judges. Andretti. They were all scumbags. What you did is perfectly understandable. You...."

"Get real, Karen," he interrupted. "You and I both know that if I let you leave this room, you'll run to the police to spill the whole story I just told you. You'll want to get a miserable human being like me wiped off the face of the earth...."

His face was contorted. His hands shaking, his face alternated between anger and fear.

He's capable of anything right now.

"No, Cam, no," Karen rushed to say. "I don't want that. I understand why you did what you did. I really do.

"I know how painful it was for you to watch your mother suffer. You saw her happiness and good health destroyed. It was natural for you to seek vengeance against the people who did that to her. Perfectly natural, Cam. I won't go to the police. I promise I won't. I'd never go to the police....

"Davi and I will be fine," Karen added, forcing herself to smile. A reassuring smile. "I'm grateful to you for letting her go when you did. And you never really hurt her. She's fine. I guess I made things sound worse than they are. She's really okay now."

Cam's face brightened a little. Karen's empathy and her reassuring words about Davi had apparently struck a chord with him.

"I'll be going now," she said quickly. "I can walk home. I won't say a word, to the police or anyone else." Karen slowly began to rise from the sofa.

"Wait there!" he shouted. Still holding the gun in his trembling right hand, he rose, reached across the desk, and with his left hand pushed Karen back onto the sofa.

He was staring at her. A wild, crazed stare.

Could I possibly overtake him physically? I could use one of the tae kwon do techniques I learned back in Evanston. If I could just get around the desk somehow, I think I could take him down.

"I'm glad you understand," he was saying, the same crazed stare still fixed on his face. "But the rest of the world won't, don't you see? I'll be viewed as a monster, as an inhuman monster who killed out of revenge. Someone will figure out what happened, and there will be consequences.

173

Even though <u>you</u> seem to understand, the rest of the world won't. There will be consequences..."

Cam raised the gun and pointed it at Karen. She stopped breathing. Her heart was pounding. *Don't shoot me! I don't want to die!*

For a moment, no one moved.

Karen's eyes darted from his face to the gun he was holding and back.

It's time. It's time for me to risk everything. To risk that he'll shoot me. I'll move quickly to get around the desk and assume a combat position. I'll concentrate my striking force the way I learned to do.... A blow to his solar plexus, a high roundhouse kick to his head....

But as she slowly began to rise, his demeanor changed again. His crazed stare vanished, and he began to look calmly into Karen's eyes.

"Wait a minute, Karen. I know now that you aren't responsible for what happened to my mother," he said, shaking his head. "You never were. I've treated you and your daughter very badly. You didn't deserve it. It's clear to me now that your daughter...your little daughter...she needs you.

"That's why I have to do this."

Cam suddenly turned the gun towards himself, held it against his temple, and pulled the trigger.

"Cam!" Karen closed her eyes for a minute, her heart pounding so hard she thought it would jump out of her chest. Then she heard a loud thud.

174

She opened her eyes. Cam was slumped across his desk, blood running down the side of his face onto the teak desktop. His hand was still clutching the gun.

Karen tried to slow her heart rate and take a deep breath.

I know I shouldn't touch him. I should call the police. I should tell Greg....

Trembling, she rose and began to move toward the phone sitting on Cam's desk, a few inches away from his motionless body. She shakily picked up the receiver.

"This is 911. What is....?"

"I've...I've just watched someone shoot himself. I think he may be dead, but I'm not sure. Please...please send an ambulance to 2515 Jackson Street. And...please notify Lieutenant Greg Chan if you can. Tell him it's Karen Clark."

Karen was still shaking as she replaced the receiver, her heart pounding fiercely in her chest.

Finally she collapsed once more on the brown velvet sofa and waited for the ambulance to arrive.

She took a deep breath and looked outside the windows at the stunning view of the bay. The view that had looked so beautiful just a short time ago.

I'll be home soon, home with Davi. That's all that really matters.

Chapter 28

Karen heard an ambulance arrive five minutes later. She rose, stumbled to the front door of the house, and opened it.

Two EMTs briskly entered, followed her to Cam's office, and checked his vital signs. Grim-faced, they turned to Karen and shook their heads.

Cam was dead. Irretrievably, irreparably dead.

As the EMTs hoisted his body onto a stretcher and carried him off, Karen collapsed once again on the brown velvet sofa. But she felt uneasy, too uneasy to remain there. She rose and began to pace around the room, her heart pounding.

What's next? Will I hear from Greg Chan? When can I leave this dreadful house?

A minute later, Greg called her on Cam's phone. "Karen! Just got your message. Are you all right?"

Her heart was still pounding. "I'm...I'm okay, Greg," she said.

"I want to talk to you. Can you wait there for me? I can be there in five or ten minutes."

"I'll wait for you, Greg. I'm too shaken up to walk home right now. But I want to get out of here as soon as I can."

"Sure, sure," Greg said. "I understand. I'm leaving right now. Don't touch anything."

"Don't worry. I won't. But try to get here as soon as you can."

I can't wait to get out of this horrific room. This room...everything that happened here...I can't wait to leave this place and try...try to forget it.

Karen put down the phone and waited, as calmly as she could, until Greg arrived a few minutes later.

As soon as he walked in, he took Karen's hands in his. "Can I get you something? Some water? Maybe there's something else to drink. I can try to find something...."

"No, no, that's all right, Greg," she assured him. "Let's get this over with as fast as we can."

Greg nodded, seeming to understand how Karen felt. "Okay, Karen. That's exactly what we'll do." He opened his briefcase, pulled out a tape recorder, and began to record her story.

Karen spoke quickly, trying to cover all of the relevant points.

"Quite a story, Karen," Greg said when she finished. "I'll get a tech out here to collect evidence. And we'll notify the police in Chicago and La Jolla. They'll want to check their records of the deaths that took place there."

Karen nodded.

She suddenly remembered Cam's leather-covered journal, still sitting on his desk, now spattered with blood. "He told me he wrote a lot of his deranged plans in there," she said, pointing to the journal. "His list of names...."

"We'll take a close look at it," Greg said. "Thankfully, we finally know exactly what happened," he added.

"And...and...why Davi remembered 'Red Diana'."

"Right," Greg said, nodding. "Davi's a smart kid. She was smart to remember that clue. It confirms everything Harper told you."

Karen was still reeling. Her heart rate had calmed down, but her mind had not.

"I want to go home, Greg. I want to see Davi."

"Of course! What was I thinking? I'll have one of our officers drive you home."

"I can walk, Greg...."

"No, no, you're not in any shape to walk. An officer's outside, waiting for you. She'll drive you home."

"Thanks, Greg." Karen held out her hand to shake his, but Greg pulled her toward him and hugged her instead. Karen felt his body's warmth next to hers.

"You've been through a lot, Karen," he said. Releasing her, he looked into her eyes. "Go home and get some rest. You helped us get a psychopath off the street. I hope you know how brave you were to confront him. And get him to confess to all the terrible things he did. Thanks to you, he'll never threaten anyone else again."

Karen nodded weakly. She walked back through the house to the front door. It was still open, and she could see a young woman officer waving at her from an SFPD patrol car. Karen held onto the bannister as she shakily descended the seventeen green stairs to the sidewalk.

The officer whisked her into the car and drove quickly to Karen's apartment building. "Do you want me to go in with you, hon?" she asked.

"No thanks, I'll be fine," Karen said, entering the building. She was still shaky but determined to get upstairs as fast as she could.

Davi and Juanita were working on a jigsaw puzzle at the dining room table. Davi jumped up and ran over to Karen. "Mommy! I'm so glad you're home!" she said, hugging Karen.

"I'm so happy to *be* home," Karen said. "So happy to be home with you."

I won't say anything about what happened this afternoon. Not now. Not for a long time.

Juanita departed with a smile, leaving Karen and Davi alone. Hugging, they walked together to the living room and collapsed on the sofa.

"So happy...." Karen repeated.

Karen could finally say goodbye to the stress and worry she'd been living with. She could put aside her fears, her trepidation. She could at last forget the terrible specter of "Red Diana."

She no longer needed to look over her shoulder, hour after hour, day after day, filled with anguish caused by the psycho who'd terrified her and Davi. And she'd survived.

Karen and Davi had a lot to look forward to. Years of happiness, hard-won happiness, in San Francisco.

*   *   *

Two weeks later, Karen was back at work at Franklin & Cooper when her phone rang. She glanced at the caller-ID. B Hertz.

Karen's heart speeded up, but she hesitated before picking up the phone.

"Hello?" she finally said.

"Karen, it's Brad. Great news! I'm coming back to San Francisco."

Karen paused.

"I'm hoping we can see each other. I'm coming for a Friday meeting and thought I'd stay all weekend."

Karen was silent.

"I'd like to meet your daughter while I'm there. We could all go hiking together. I've heard Muir Woods is a great place to hike."

He's coming back. To see me. To meet Davi.

"Karen?"

"Yes, Brad," she said. "That sounds great. When do you plan to get here?"

Karen sat back in her black leather chair and listened to Brad's plans.

Sunlight was coming through her window, and life suddenly seemed to offer all sorts of possibilities.

ACKNOWLEDGMENTS

My profound gratitude goes, as always, to my daughters, Meredith and Leslie, for their boundless help and encouragement. Special thanks to Meredith, who assisted me so brilliantly throughout the entire process.

I'm also grateful to the wonderful friends who read one of my drafts and offered me a host of helpful suggestions: Ron Yank, Jocelyn Startz, Susan Pollack, Christine H. Davis, John Davis, and Michael Sorgen.

Thanks also to my delightful consultant on tae kwon do: my astonishing granddaughter, Elizabeth Helen.

Finally, this book is dedicated to Herb, who was a constant source of love, support, and encouragement during the extraordinary life we shared. He remains forever in my heart.

"I carry your heart with me/I carry it in my heart" - e.e.cummings

ABOUT THE AUTHOR

Susan Alexander is a graduate of Harvard Law School who has worked as a lawyer in the public interest, along with serving as a federal judge's law clerk, an arbitrator, a law school professor, and a consultant on legal writing. She has also worked at three Chicago law firms. She earned her AB with highest honors from Washington University in St. Louis and an MA in political science from Northwestern University.

Susan now focuses primarily on writing. Her writing has appeared in a wide array of publications, including the San Francisco Chronicle, the Chicago Tribune, the Chicago Sun-Times, the Chicago Daily Law Bulletin, the San Francisco Daily Journal, the Los Angeles Daily Journal, the Baltimore Sun, the New York Daily News, the ABA Journal, and a host of other professional and mainstream publications. She was the first editor of *The Almanac of the Federal Judiciary,* and her short story "Neglect" was a winner in Chicago Lawyer magazine's first annual fiction competition.

Susan Alexander lives in San Francisco. Her first novel featuring Karen Clark, *A Quicker Blood,* was published in 2009 to wide acclaim. Her second novel, *Jealous Mistress,* also earning high praise, was published in 2011.

You can visit Susan's website at susanalexander.com. Her blog, *Susan Just Writes,* has published her comments on a wide variety of topics once a month since 2012.

AUTHOR'S NOTE

This story is total fiction, but much of it stems from things that have happened to me in real life.

I wanted to highlight three themes: the shattering pain of loss, the terrible burden of guilt, and the powerful desire for revenge.

The desire for revenge, in particular, strikes me as a natural human reaction to believing that one has been wronged. This desire for revenge plays an important part in my story.

Two very different views of the law and lawyers are set forth by two of the story's major characters. My hope is that this story helps readers become aware of the many flaws in our system of "justice" and the profound impact these flaws can have on those who get caught up in it.

A life-altering injury to an elderly person, and its aftermath—similar to those described in this story--happened to someone very close to me.

To the reader: *RED DIANA* includes a brief mention of what happened to Karen in Walden, Wisconsin. The whole story appears in an earlier novel, *A Quicker Blood.* Now that you've read *Red Diana,* you may want to learn the whole story by reading *A Quicker Blood.*

Finally, <u>a spoiler alert</u>: The inspiration for the title "RED DIANA" (and the clue my protagonist pursued) was my daughter Meredith's Harvard diploma. Standing in the doorway of Meredith's bedroom, I glimpsed a frame propped against a wall. The frame was resting on the floor, surrounded by loose fragments of other stuff that covered most of what the frame enclosed. When I tried to figure out what was inside the frame, I could decipher only "DIANA," the last part of Harvard's Latin name (HARVARDIANA) as it appeared at the top of the diploma, and the middle three letters in Meredith's name, "RED."

That led me to create the story of "RED DIANA."

QUESTIONS FOR DISCUSSION

1. When Karen finds Davi the morning after her abduction, how does Karen initially react to seeing Davi? Why do you think she reacts that way? Do you think you would react the same way in a similar situation?

2. After Karen returns to work, what is her most overwhelming emotion? Do you think you would feel the same emotion? Why or why not?

3. What did you think of the description of Karen's life in New York City? Did the description of the life of a Wall Street lawyer like her surprise you?

4. What did you think of Karen's response to losing Jon? Can you compare it to the responses of people you know to the loss of their loved ones?

5. Karen had difficulty adjusting to life without Jon. Do you think she could have done more to make her new life happier? How?

6. What did you think of Lisa Robbins's attempts to encourage her friend Karen to move to San Francisco? Would you try to encourage

a friend to move to a new city, as Lisa did? Or would you do something else to help him or her?

7. Karen tried to think of explanations for the clues "Diana" and "Red Diana." Which of her ideas seemed the most promising? Why? If you were a friend of hers, would you have suggested other possible explanations?

8. When Cam tells his story to Karen, he occasionally paused to look out his windows at his view of San Francisco Bay and the Golden Gate Bridge. He would also pause to do something else—something that has largely gone out of fashion. What was it? Do you know anyone who still does it?

9. What did you think of Karen's sudden reconnection with her classmate Brad? Would you consider reconnecting with an attractive person from your past in a similar way?

10. Karen encounters psychopaths in two different cities, and she manages to survive both of them in spite of the threat they posed to her. What would you do if you encountered a psycho who posed a threat to you?

11. Cam believed that his beloved mother had been seriously injured by Morris Andretti. How did Cam react to learning what Andretti did? Would you react the same way?

12. Cam's view of the law and lawyers was colored by the way they treated his mother's lawsuit. If you had a loved one who was injured by someone like Andretti, would you think about filing a lawsuit that would hold him/her responsible?

13. If you didn't get satisfaction from your lawsuit, would you become embittered and try to seek what you viewed as "justice" another way? How?

14. Do you think that some of the lawyers in the story acted unethically or inappropriately? What about the judges?

15. We need to believe that there are lawyers and judges who conduct themselves ethically and appropriately. Do you think that Karen is an example of a lawyer who appears to conduct herself ethically and appropriately?

16. Did this story change your view of lawyers, judges, and our legal system?